MW01299112

mine forever

SPECIAL EDITION

THE CAPE SANDS SERIES
BOOK 2

ELIZA PEAKE

Lucretia,
Enjoy Chase & Eden!
Happy Reading & Stay Spicy!
XOXO,
Eliza Peake

CAPTIVATED WORDS
PUBLISHING

MINE FOREVER - SPECIAL EDITION

By Eliza Peake

ISBN #: 978-1-960124-25-8

Editor: Happily Editing Anns, Atlanta

Proofreading by: Happily Editing Anns, Atlanta

Cover Design by: Heart to Cover - Julianne Fangmann, New York

www.elizapeake.com

Created with Vellum

author note

Thank you so much for taking a chance on Mine Forever. I love this story and this hero so much, but there is some content that may be triggering for some.

The following topics are mentioned in the book and may be considered sensitive: emotional child abuse (off page), death of a spouse (off page), and a car accident (on page).

ONE
eden

EVER HAVE a day where the feeling of foreboding is so strong that going back to bed, pulling the covers over your head, and turning on *The Golden Girls* is the only sane option?

Yeah, me too.

Today's that day.

First, I oversleep, something I never do.

Then, the zipper on my favorite pencil skirt breaks.

Followed by dropping the mascara wand on my white blouse.

Next obstacle—the second elevator in my well-placed apartment building in Lennox Hill is on the fritz, which means it takes me twice as long to get out of the building.

My local barista can't do me wrong, right?

Wrong.

I pick up my venti vanilla latte with three espresso shots, only to find on the train ride to my small but well-placed office in Midtown Manhattan that it's a chai tea.

I hate chai tea.

The twitch camped out between my shoulder blades since I woke up doesn't let up as I walk through the door of my office.

"Eden, Mason Jackstone's agent's on the phone."

Katie, my assistant, pokes her head into my minimally decorated office with a deep frown on her face that makes my stomach turn.

"Thanks." I plaster a smile on my face to hide the nerves in my voice as I pick up the phone. "Barb, how are you today?"

The sigh from the other end is heavy, and that twitch shifts into full throttle. "Eden, I'm sure you've seen the news."

I roll my shoulders. "Um, no. It's been a busy morning."

Another heavy sigh. "Mason had an accident on his motorcycle. He's going to be in the hospital for at least a week, maybe longer if he needs another surgery. Obviously, he's unable to speak at the charity ball."

And there it is.

Fuck my life.

The bad feeling I'd fought all morning has come to fruition.

"Oh my God! Is there anything I can do?"

"I don't think so. He has a mild concussion and some bad road rash. The biggest thing is his leg and arm. In the long run, he'll be okay. But it's going to take some time." Barb pauses. "I'm so sorry, Eden. I know this is last minute."

"I'm just glad Mason is okay. Don't worry about me. I'll find a replacement." I inject enthusiasm I don't feel into the words.

I *am* happy he's alive—I'm not a monster.

After a few moments, Barb and I say our goodbyes, and I lean back in my gently used office chair, trying not to have a complete meltdown.

Mason Jackstone is *the* it guy right now in the world of sports. And the trio of New York football players turned real estate billionaires that hired my company, Perfection Planning, to manage their event are all extreme sports junkies.

Mason was the perfect fit for them.

And now the one ace I had in the hole is gone.

Not only is this charity ball one of the most talked about events of the year, but it's also the only thing that stands between me and bankruptcy.

If I don't pull off this event, I can't pay the balloon payment on my loan.

If I don't pay the loan, I lose everything. Including the team of fifteen people I treasure and that depend on me for their livelihoods.

I'm not a huge corporation, but I have a decent-sized business and pay my people well for the work they do. We all work hard and reap the rewards.

At least, that had been the idea when I started the company and hired my employees.

Still, we're a family and I need to take care of them.

Unfortunately, I went to college and got a PR degree, not a business degree, so I've learned some lessons from the school of hard knocks.

Money management being top of the list.

Katie walks in with her pale pink "cat mom" mug, a tendril of steam rising from it. "Mason's out?" she asks, sinking down in the chair on the other side of my desk.

I sigh. "Yeah."

She nods. "I figured as much after I saw the article about his accident."

"How did I not hear about this?"

She flips a lock of her rose-gold hair over her shoulder. "Don't you watch the news?"

I roll my eyes. "Yes, I watch the news. Current events, world issues, the weather. What I don't watch is the E! News channel."

She sips her coffee. "Well, see? You should. If you did, you'd know he was hit by a certain Hollywood starlet who's drinking again and nearly killed him. Nasty accident."

I rub my forehead to ward off the marching band setting up behind my eyes. "Well, send a gift to Barb so it will get to him. Bottle of whiskey or something."

"I'll figure it out."

And she'd no doubt make me look good, like always. She's a gem, in spite of her irrational love for the color pink and a wardrobe that makes her look like she stepped out of the fifties.

I lean my head back and sigh, turning my chair toward the window. It isn't a big window, but the location and view are worth every penny of the exorbitant rent I pay.

Tears well up in my eyes, and I blink hard against them.

No time for tears, Eden. Real Mitchells don't cry.

Yes, Mama. I'm sorry.

I clear my throat and face Katie. "Okay, we need a name that's going to draw a big crowd, preferably someone in the sports realm, like Mason. These guys want donations, so we need to bring someone in that will lighten the deep pockets of those coming to the event."

Lost in thought, I sip from my cup and almost gag, forgetting it's chai tea. "Can you get me some coffee? I ended up with someone's chai tea."

"On it."

When she comes back with my coffee, she rattles off a couple of movie stars we've worked with in the past, a well-known motivational speaker, and a retired basketball player that would still draw in the high rollers.

"Yeah, we're not getting any of those this late in the game." My nerves spark under my skin, and I need to move. Pacing my office, all I can think of is complete blanks.

"I know you aren't going to like this suggestion," Katie says, "but I know who would be perfect for this if available."

I raise my head, frowning. "Who?"

"Hollywood Hanover."

My eyes bulge. "Chase Hanover? As in my ex, Chase Hanover?"

Katie picks imaginary lint off her white and pink polka-dotted skirt, her eyes averted. "I was thinking more along the lines of Hollywood Hanover, former major league baseball superstar."

"No."

"You know, the elusive Hollywood Hanover that everyone is *still* trying to interview since his retirement a few years ago."

I roll my eyes. I hate the ridiculous nickname the media gave him. "No. Hard pass," I say. "Besides, even if we could find him, he wouldn't do it anyway."

"Why not?"

I sit with a thump in my chair, tightness spreading across my chest. "The last time I saw Chase was four years ago after the memorial service. We haven't spoken since."

"Okay, that happens sometimes. Time passes, etc."

I shift in my chair. "Yeah, well we didn't exactly part on great terms."

That night plays rent free in my head more often than it should. So many emotions filled that night.

"Do you know where he is now?"

"Last I knew he'd moved to Florida. But I don't know." I'd made it clear I didn't want to know since I never returned his calls.

But I have a pretty good idea where he landed, and I know who can tell me.

She rises and shuts the door before coming to sit on the edge of my desk.

"Look, I don't know what went on between you and Chase, but this is business. It can't hurt to try. If he says no..." She bobs her head from side to side. "We'll cross that bridge if we get to it."

My assistant's right—this is business. Emotions have no place here. I can't let a little thing like him being the one that got away interfere with my livelihood.

I can do this.

I *have* to do this.

Regret knots up in my gut, but time's running out and so are my choices.

"Okay, fine. I'll talk to Chase."

"Good. How can I help?"

"Find me Liz Fallon's number."

The more I think about it, the more I warm up to it, and adrenaline courses through my veins.

I rattle off more instructions for her including travel arrangements for first thing in the morning and to rearrange my schedule.

"Call an emergency staff meeting. I'll talk with the team about the proposal and what's going on."

"Will do." Katie chews her lip, then rubs her nose.

Aw, shit. Her bad news tell. "What is it?"

"You know there's a tropical storm headed toward Florida, right?"

I type out an email, half listening. "Yeah, I heard about it. But it's bound to happen. It is October after all and still hurricane season. It's fine though. It's still a couple of days away, and they're predicting it will move out over the Atlantic anyway. It'll be fine. As long as the Jacksonville airport is open, I'm going and it'll be fine."

"If you're sure..."

"Everything is going to be fine."

TWO
eden

NOTHING IS FINE.

Less than five minutes with my heels on the ground in the Sunshine State and I'm rethinking my strategy.

I'm lucky that Liz, Chase's agent, took my call. But we've always had a good working relationship, and she told me several times Chase needed me.

No way. I spent years trying to do that. I'm no longer in the business of saving Chase.

I'd gone down with that ship years ago.

Liz hadn't been sure if he was on the island right now, but his last known address she had was Cape Sands Beach.

I don't have time to waste and yet here I am, waiting in line to pick up a rental car in the Jacksonville airport.

Liz may not have been sure, but my gut tells me he's here right now. Although I'm not sure I can trust it where Chase Hanover is concerned.

I've made too many mistakes that have cost me more than I can think about when it comes to this man.

The chipper rental car clerk checks me in quickly, and with

light traffic through Jacksonville and St. Augustine, I'm nearing the charming little beach town of Cape Sands in record time.

I head south toward the bridge that leads over to Cape Sands Beach, and when it comes into sight, I blow out a breath and tighten my hands on the wheel.

"You can do this, Mitchell. You're a professional. You're no longer a college girl in awe of the college baseball star."

Right. Sure.

I never think of Chase or the way he once meant everything to me.

As long as dreams don't count.

I'm here strictly for business.

I'm not here to make friends, to see how he's doing, or comfort him in any way.

Comforting him is a mistake I'm definitely not repeating again.

I roll down the windows, and the briny sea air fills the cabin of the SUV.

But one deep inhale brings back memories that I'd rather forget.

The windows go back up.

There's only one way to survive the short amount of time I'm here and that's to block out all the memories that threaten to break free and torment me.

If I lose sight of my goal, I'm finished.

Staying professional is the way to handle it. Which also means kneeing the asshole in the balls is out.

The wide bridge gives way to a two-lane road running through a little town area that embraces an eclectic mix of vintage, contemporary, and beachy.

My sigh of relief is deep when I see a coffee shop. The early morning coffee buzz wore off hours ago, and I need a pick-me-up to feel human before I see my ex face-to-face.

And proceed to beg with class and dignity.

I wish I knew who I'd pissed off in another life that has landed me in this situation.

When anxiety claws at me, I think about what's at stake. Not just my livelihood, but the financial lives of Katie and all my other workers.

Promises had been made to them, and failing my people isn't an option.

And if that means facing my past head-on, then I'll do it. Even if the anxiety makes me want to lose what little breakfast I ate.

I park in a public parking lot next to the row of buildings housing the coffee shop and step out into a wall of humidity that makes my clothes stick to me immediately.

Walking into the coffee shop, I find an air-conditioned, caffeinated heaven with the rich aroma of java that promises to pack the punch I need.

Judging by the line, it looks like the whole town is looking for their caffeine fix.

I shift my stance and do my best not to push along the woman at the counter telling the barista that her granddaughter finally graduated from the bottle to a sippy cup.

"It's a whole different pace around here," a deep voice says near my ear.

Startled, I turn around and stare into the face of a man who can give Chase a run for his money in the "Hey, I'm hot and broody" category.

And is as famous as Chase in his own right.

"I'm sorry, what?"

He chuckles and the smile I've seen in advertisements makes an appearance. "Well, I can tell you're not from here. The reason it's slow is because Ms. Odette up there"—he nods with his strong chin—"is telling Becky all about the new baby."

"Oh, yes. Well, thanks."

"No problem."

I face forward again, before turning back to him. "How did you know I'm not from here?"

He waves a hand up and down. "The outfit."

"What's wrong with it?"

"Nothing. It just doesn't scream island time."

I look down at my trademark work uniform of a button-up blouse and pencil skirt. A glance around the shop tells me I couldn't look more out of place if I'd run through the coffee shop with my hair on fire.

"I suppose it doesn't," I say with a smile.

"Hey, there's a smile." He holds out a hand. "Nate Gentry."

"Yeah, I know who you are," I say, shaking his hand. "Eden Mitchell."

"Are you a fan of baseball, Eden?"

If he only knew...

"I've seen a game or two. But you're all over the place, so..."

He smiles. "Yeah, but it should slow down now."

As we move forward, I glance back. "You live on the island now?"

He holds a finger up to his lips and winks. "Shhh...don't tell anyone."

"How did you know that woman's name was Odette?"

He chuckles. "Everyone knows Odette."

"Ahhh...yes. Small towns."

"What about you? What brings you to the island? It's kinda lousy timing. There's a storm coming in."

"I plan to be out of here by tomorrow. Sooner, if I can find a...friend of mine."

"Oh yeah? Who are you looking for? I may be able to help."

"Chase Hanover?"

"Seriously?"

"You know him?"

He chuckles. "He's my neighbor."

My breath catches. Holy shit. I found him.

Is my luck finally turning?

"Wow, small world."

He gestures behind me. "Becky's ready for you."

"Oh,"—I turn to face the barista—"I'd like a large vanilla latte, extra hot, triple shot."

"Sure thing."

"Can you add Eden's to my order and I'll take two large coffees, black."

The young girl nods. "Sure thing."

Before I can protest for Nate generously paying for my coffee, it's rung up and paid.

I smile at him as we move to the designated waiting area. "Thanks for that. You didn't have to buy my coffee."

He shrugs. "No big deal. It's just a coffee."

"So, do you happen to know where Chase is right now?"

"He's told me he'd be at one of his properties getting it storm ready." He tilts his head. "How long have you and Hanover been friends?"

"Since college."

"Ah, college sweethearts?"

Thankfully, before I have to answer or dodge that question, our names are called. Once we get our coffees, he holds the door open for me as we leave.

"I'm headed there now, if you want to follow me."

When he pulls his truck out and heads onto the main highway, I follow him, trying to figure out what I'll say when I see Chase.

"Hey, Chase. Remember me? You know, the big mistake you made?"

Yeah, that's not going to go over well.

Sighing, I look around, hoping the sand or beach houses will give me some inspiration.

"Let's see... Chase, good to see you..." I shake my head. "Ah, Eden, let's keep the lies to a minimum, okay?"

My head keeps reminding me of the last words we said to each other. Anger and hurt ran deep between us.

But my heart?

That stupid bitch is pounding at the thought of seeing him again. The way it always did when I knew I was going to see him.

My stomach flip-flops, but I shut down all the memories that will do nothing but threaten any bravado I've mustered to come here.

The farther down the island, the farther apart the houses become until we reach a dead end to the road.

Nate takes a left onto a street with just a handful of houses. To my right, the Atlantic stretches out in all its mysterious deep blue beauty.

The only sign a storm is on its way are the winds that have picked up a bit. But the blue skies are promising that I can get what I need—for Chase to say yes—and get my ass on the next plane back to New York.

My confidence about Chase's reaction to my request isn't as promising as the skies, though.

Nate pulls his truck into a short, crushed-shell driveway of a beach home on stilts behind a blacked-out truck.

Chase isn't anywhere to be seen, and with the house looking deserted, if Nate wasn't who he is, I'd start to wonder why I followed him.

Parking on the street in front of the house, I stall for a

moment before blowing out a breath and getting out of the rental. Between the oppressive humidity and my nerves, nausea roils in my stomach

Squaring my shoulders, I head in the direction where Nate went. As I approach, the ocean winds blowing around me, I hear a couple of male voices though I can't hear what they're saying.

As I round the corner, Nate says, "I brought you something,"

"As grateful as I am for the coffee, I hope like hell it's a six-pack of beer."

I freeze, the click of my heels on the concrete silenced.

I haven't heard his voice in four years, but it affects me just the same. That deep-timbered rasp caresses my skin like a lover's touch.

Nate chuckles and squints up to the side of the house where the ladder leans against it. "Better. Bring your ass down here and see for yourself."

The ladder creaks and jostles. Work boots hit the rungs, followed by jean-clad legs. I nearly swallow my tongue as that sexy-as-hell happy trail comes into view when his T-shirt rides up.

All the times I ever touched that happy trail—with my fingertips or my tongue—play in my head, making it feel about two hundred degrees out here.

"What did you—"

Chase stops when he looks over at me. His worn and faded baseball cap—his lucky Gators cap—is pulled low, but it doesn't hide the flash of anger in those emerald-green eyes.

His hands land on his hips, back ramrod straight. Those lips—my body recalls just how perfect they felt on my skin—flatten into a straight line.

Maybe I should have broken my sex drought before I came

here. Because the anger I wanted to hang on to so desperately has abandoned me.

"Is this a joke, Gentry?" Chase's voice is tight and cold enough to freeze over the ocean just beyond the house.

Nate looks back and forth between us, confusion written on his face. "This is Eden Mitchell."

"I know who the hell she is."

"She says you're friends."

"She fucking lied."

THREE
chase

I'M GOING to kill Nate.

He's just the messenger, but that's his bad luck.

I don't want to be staring at Eden Mitchell right now. It fucks with my head whenever I see her.

Just when I finally feel like I'm starting to put my life back together and find my little bit of peace here in Cape Sands, Eden Mitchell shows up.

How the hell did she find me anyway?

"Hello, Chase."

Her voice is controlled, cultured in a way it wasn't a few years ago. It's sexy as hell and rubs me the wrong way.

She's changed her hair since I last saw her. It's longer, brushing past her shoulders. Where it once reminded me of dark, smooth caramel, now it reminds me of honey.

And her eyes?

Fuck, those eyes have always been my undoing. All the greens and blues that swirl in them. Depending on her mood, some colors are more prominent than others.

Right now, they're a dark blue and wary.

Shake it off, Hanover. You sound like a damn pussy waxing poetic over her eyes and comparing her hair to food.

"What do you want, Eden?"

"I want to talk to you."

"What could we possibly have to talk about?" I narrow my eyes and cross my arms over my chest. "Did Liz send you out here?"

For the last few weeks, my agent has been trying to get me on the phone for more than five minutes.

And while she's the best agent in the business, I'm going to fire her ass as soon as possible if she helped Eden find me.

It would be just like her to do that as a way to get me to call her.

"No. But I do have some business I'd like to discuss with you."

"Business, huh?" The muscle in my cheek tics, and my jaw clenches. If I don't let up, I'll break a tooth.

Nate clears his throat and starts to back away. "You know what? I'm starving. I think I'll head back to see...yeah..."

I don't respond, unsure of what will spew out of my mouth that I'll be sorry for later.

Nate drives off a few moments later, and there's nothing but sounds of the wind and seagulls between us.

"I don't care what business you want to discuss, Eden. I can't help you. There's your answer. Now get the hell off my property."

"I'm not leaving, Chase. Not until you hear me out." She straightens her spine and drops her hands to her hips. "You owe me at least that much."

My gaze flits down to her chest where her blouse stretches across her breasts that move up and down with her breaths. Breasts that I...

No, damn it!

I focus on her words and let the angry part of me lead the way.

My eyes snap back to hers. "Owe you? I don't owe anyone anything, Eden. You'd do best to remember that."

That isn't entirely true.

We've done our fair share of hurting each other, and my actions are no small part of that.

I should try to hear her out, but I know what will happen if she's around me for too long.

She's my fucking kryptonite, and I'm no superhero.

Her eyes flash green fire, and the defiant look in them makes the blood rush to my dick.

Fucking A.

"I'd do best to remember that? Who the fuck do you think you're talking to, Hanover? I'm not some minion on your team or one of your little groupies."

My palms itch to touch her.

I scoff. "I remember once upon a time when you loved being my personal groupie, Sunshine."

Silence hangs heavy between us.

It's a shitty thing to say, no matter how I feel about her now. And I don't mean it in the way it came out.

I hate how the nickname I'd given her in college slips off my tongue, and I want to take that back too.

Nicknames like that signal affection, and I don't have the capacity to give any woman—but especially this one—that sort of thing.

I put my hands on my hips and look down for a moment. After a couple of deep breaths, I lift my head to meet her angry gaze. "Eden, level with me. What do you want?"

She continues to stare at me for a moment before clearing her throat. "My company was hired by a group to plan and coordinate a charity ball. Big names, high rollers. But my A-list keynote speaker is now...indisposed."

"And you want me to be your keynote speaker."

"Yes."

"No."

I walk toward the ladder and bend down to gather my tools.

She's hot on my heels. "What do you mean, no?"

I raise up and look her in the eye. "As in the opposite of yes."

"But you barely listened to me."

I place the drill in the tool bag and hoist it up.

Pain radiates down my arm, but I keep the wince off my face. I'd overdone it today and my shoulder is protesting.

Loudly.

"Sure I did. You lost your keynote speaker and you want me to take his place. Bail you out. I said no." I raise a brow and smirk. "I think it's pretty simple. But then, you always were the queen of complicated."

Damn, she really can bring out the asshole in me. But I need to push her away, send her back to New York. Get her the fuck off my island.

Four years isn't long enough to get her out of my system since I can't continue to look at her and not want to touch her.

She's my own personal heaven and hell all rolled into one.

Why the hell does she want me to be her speaker anyway? I'm a bad bet and we both know it.

I walk past her toward my truck, pushing away the stab in my chest when hurt flashes through her eyes just before anger settles back in.

And fuck, if she doesn't smell the same as she always had, a heady mix of vanilla and amber. Rich with just a touch of sweetness.

I don't even want to think about if she tastes the same.

"Chase." Eden follows me to the back of the truck, where I lift the tool bag over the side and drop it in with a loud clatter.

"What?" I ask, turning back to her. I roll my shoulders in an effort to keep the pain in my right one from taking me out.

"The least you could do is hear me out. Let me tell you the whole story." The sun shines onto her hair, lighting up the blonde-colored strands. "I don't like mixing business and personal—"

"Then don't."

She sighs heavily and looks away for a moment, before bringing her gaze back to mine. "I'd owe you big. Please. Just listen to what I have to say?"

"What more could you have to say? You asked; I said no."

She rubs her forehead, and that vertical line between her eyes tells me she's mentally counting to ten.

"Let me just give you all the details before you totally shut me down. I promise I won't take much of your time."

I search her eyes for anything that signals she's putting me on. But all I find is determination with a side helping of desperation.

Shit.

I never could say no to this woman, not since the day I met her. That's part of my problem when it comes to her.

I twirl my keys on my index finger, looking away. There's no way in hell I'm ever going back to the city that's ground zero to the demise of my career and personal life.

But listening to why she's here seems to be the only way to get her back over the bridge and out of my life.

"If I listen, will that get you on a plane back to New York any faster?"

Quiet for a moment, she finally says with a nod, "Yes."

"Okay, fine." I jerk open the driver's side door and slide in.

"Meet me at my house at three. I'll hear you out, but my answer won't change."

I slam the door to put some steel between us.

She moves closer to the open window. The breeze catches at that moment, and her unique scent tickles my senses.

"Thank you, Chase." When I start the engine and drop it into gear, her eyes widen. "Wait, where's your house?"

I smirk. "You have a way of finding out things, Eden. I'm sure you'll figure it out. I gotta go."

With my chin, I nod in the direction of her SUV. "You might want to go ahead and move that monstrosity of a vehicle off the curb. I don't want to have to help you out if you get stuck in the sand."

She rolls her eyes and makes a noise that resembles a growl but walks away without another word.

In the side mirror, I watch her stalk back to her vehicle.

My gaze stays on her ass and legs that look a million miles long in those sexy-as-fuck heels. I lean my head back and close my eyes.

I'm in so much fucking trouble.

Again.

FOUR

chase

A COUPLE OF HOURS LATER, the four properties I own on the island are ready for whatever the incoming storm has to offer.

I drive along the beachfront road, and glancing around, it looks like a storm would be the last thing to worry about with the sunshine and high white clouds.

But the winds are picking up and the sea is beginning to get choppy. Far out on the horizon, purple clouds are beginning to show themselves, making the air heavy.

At the rate the storm is moving and growing, it won't be long before we see how bad it is.

The dashboard clock says I have a little over an hour until Eden will be at my house.

Knowing her, she'll be early, and since my own place needs some prep work, I point the truck toward the end of the island.

My stomach is in knots with the thoughts of having Eden near my sanctuary.

Why the hell did I say to meet at my house?

Just one more time I weaken for her even when I think I'm in control.

All I want is to be left alone on the island that's my saving grace. Live out my days in the sun, managing my properties and keeping up with the handyman business I'd started to keep me busy.

Be that grumpy old bastard sitting at the end of the bar, watching the out-of-towners bake themselves like lobsters and drop a month's worth of pay into our local economy.

I don't date or go out much on purpose. Sure, I'm still a guy and want to get laid on occasion. I injured my million-dollar arm, not my dick.

But the truth is, I haven't gotten laid in over six months. A long-ass time for the guy who'd once had any willing woman at the snap of my fingers.

I'd had a "friends with benefits" arrangement with a local woman for a while, but she moved to Miami six months ago. Since then, it's been just me and my hand.

But I'm content to leave my celebrity back on the mainland —*even though high season on the island brings out the cleat chasers* —and simply be a guy who fixes things around town and is a respectable, contributing member of the community.

I enjoy drinking a beer sitting on my back deck overlooking the Atlantic, being out of the limelight, and not dealing with the dating scene.

It was part of the reason my arrangement with Tess had worked so well before she moved.

Was I alone? Sure.

Was I lonely? It didn't matter. I had everything I needed.

Whenever I'd wanted more, it had always blown up in my face. The last time I tried having more, it was built on lies, had ended two lives, and my career had gone down in flames.

I'm disinclined to try again with any woman. Even the one who still owns me all these years later.

A weight lifts off my shoulders when the land dotted with houses and condos becomes open beach and trees.

It means home is near.

At the very tip of Cape Sands Beach, I built my fortress.

Surrounded by oak and palm trees on one side, the Atlantic on the south side, and the Intracoastal Waterway on the north side, it isn't like I can't be found.

But I don't make it easy with the high white block walls and wrought iron security gate, not to mention the best hidden camera and security system money can buy on my property.

It may sound like overkill, but after everything that happened four years ago, the paparazzi has been insane.

Even though I'm not a celebrity athlete anymore and most of the vultures have lost interest, occasionally a stray one shows up looking for a morsel to dig up the scandal again.

Moments later, I open the door to the house and sigh in relief. The cool air surrounds me and chills my overheated skin.

After toeing off my boots at the door, I wander into the kitchen in search of a cold beer.

My stomach growls at the lack of contents in my big-ass fridge. My housekeeper, Louise, usually keeps the fridge stocked, but she's been gone for two weeks visiting her grandkids in North Carolina. And with the impending storm, I told her to wait until it passed before she heads back.

But there's still beer left, which is just what I need.

I plop down on the couch and crack open the bottle, taking a long, deep drink, relishing the bite of the cold carbonation on my throat.

Closing my eyes, I lean my head back on the cushion. With each sip, my body relaxes little by little.

But my mind is a jumble of images, the past and present mixing together, most of them with Eden Mitchell front and center.

The first day we met.

All the times we spent at the beach on spring break.

All of the times my body sank into hers and the little sighs she made when I moved inside her.

Leaving her for the big leagues and promising I'd be back.

A promise I wanted to keep but didn't.

After that it all went black.

Except for the screams and the smell of burning rubber among other things. The ass over teakettle motion that made me feel like I was flying through the air...

"Hey, man. Wake up."

I swing at the motion, at the feel of being held down and flying at the same time.

"Chase, wake up!"

My eyes spring open to find Nate Gentry in front of me, holding my arms down.

Son of a bitch, the fucker's strong.

I blink, trying to clear the cobwebs and the bad memories out of my mind. I swallow hard against the desert in my throat. "Uh, sorry."

I attempt to move out of his grip on my shoulders, but he doesn't budge. He lifts a brow. "You good?"

"I'm good."

He releases me and picks up one of the beers he'd set on the coffee table. "I see you already started."

I lift my bottle to my lips to drink away the bitterness on my tongue. "Yeah."

"What's going on, man?"

"What do you mean?"

"You were a bit more hostile than normal with Eden. Which is saying something for you."

"I have my reasons." I tip the bottle back only to find it empty.

He settles back into the couch, eyeing me. "I've got all day. So, go on. Tell me your reasons."

I start peeling the label off the beer bottle. "Let's not and say we did."

"Okay, that's fine."

But instead of getting up and leaving me in my misery, he just turns his head and looks out the wall of windows.

"Don't you have practice to go to or a commercial to film or something other than sitting here bothering me?"

A grin splits his face. "Not right now."

I've known Nate since the minor leagues.

I was an up-and-coming pitcher for the New York Admirals, and he was the hot new catcher heading to the Cape Sands major league team, the Bull Sharks. Our teams have faced off over the years and we've stayed friendly.

He's one of the few guys I know that hates many of the trappings that come with the fame and fortune, especially the media and the cleat chasers that try to trap him.

And because of that, the media often don't know if they love him or find him to be a broody SOB.

So when my career imploded, he's one of the few players that wasn't afraid to stand by me and remind me what bullshit all of this can be.

He's the guy who found me this piece of land and why I decided to make the move to Cape Sands.

Nate Gentry is one of the most stand-up guys I know. I owe him a great deal.

And I trust him.

But even he doesn't know much about Eden. The only time I've ever mentioned Eden to him is when we got drunk one night and I mentioned how the girl I was seeing at the time reminded me of Eden.

When I sobered up, I started dating brunettes only.

I sigh and drop my head back on the cushion.

"Eden and I met in college. We dated for a few years and then I went to the minors. We parted ways and that's that."

"That's that? I call bullshit."

"Yeah, well, fuck you."

He chuckles, unperturbed by my little snit. "Why do I feel like there's more to this story?"

"Because you're an arrogant prick?"

He nods as he sips his beer. "That has been mentioned a time or two," he says after he swallows, "but I'm also right, aren't I?"

I sigh again. "Fine. I was in love with her. But I fucked it up when I left. When I got to the majors, it was good PR for me to be the bachelor stud. You know how it is."

He frowns. "Yeah, unfortunately I do."

"Then I married Heather, and the PR machine spun that the way they wanted to and I fell right into it again."

I sip my beer, but let the memories of my wedding day play in my head.

In spite of the fact I know now I never truly loved Heather, it had been a good day.

"Y'all had a great wedding, man."

I nod for a moment before I can find my voice. "Heather was beautiful."

I look down and finish peeling the label off the bottle before sticking the paper inside. "But I never should have married her. For a lot of reasons, but the biggest one being I didn't love her." I scrub my face with one hand.

"Still, that doesn't mean she—"

"Leave it, Nate. You're right. But I drove Heather to do what she did. It was my fault."

I look out toward the backyard where the waves are starting to grow and the wind continues to pick up. "Look, I'd love to continue spilling my guts to you, but I have work to do before the storm comes in. Plus I gotta get some food."

I stand and Nate follows.

"I'll help you."

I shake my head. I need his help, but I need to have some alone time more.

My head has to be right before Eden arrives. "Nah, it won't take me long, but I need to get started."

"You sure? I can work on the garage while you get the guest house. Or I can go pull the boat up out of the water."

I laugh. "The boat's on a hydraulic lift, and the guest house has hurricane shutters. All I need to do is the garage, and I think I can handle it. Go home and leave me alone."

"Fine, fine. Can't say I didn't try."

After he leaves, I get to work covering the windows of the detached garage where I house a couple of toys I still own from my baseball days—my Harley and a 1965 Corvette.

I drive screws into plywood, and the mindless work has me thinking back to what my life was like a few years ago.

It's fall and if we're still playing, it means we had a great season and are in the playoffs.

Signing autographs.

Fending off the women.

But in my last year before retiring, it hadn't been as carefree.

My late wife turned heads, and when I saw guys flirting with her, I'd had my suspicions she hadn't been fending off the guys at all.

But honestly, I'd been too wrapped up in my career to pay attention.

I had one love at the time, and it wasn't Heather.

Baseball has always been a demanding and greedy mistress, about as greedy and demanding as Heather had been.

Not to mention I gave my heart away a long time ago and never got it back.

Eden's face swims into the forefront of my mind's eye.

She'd been the only woman I'd loved more than baseball.

And yet, that isn't exactly true either, is it?

I worked my ass off to be the best in the league, one of the best in history some said. Baseball had been the one love that never let me down. It had always been there.

Until it wasn't.

I have more money than I'll ever be able to spend, a beautiful house in a small slice of paradise, and my life is my own. Isn't that what most people would call living your best life?

The reality is those are just things that don't really matter.

I learned too late that the things that do matter are gone. My wife is dead, the love of my life hates me, and the range of motion in my arm has left me with the ability to swing a hammer—but I'll never be able to throw my trademark fastball again.

I'd come to Cape Sands to get away from my life and anything that reminded me of what I'd lost. Here, there is peace. No one bothers me for the most part.

My celebrity lost its luster about six months after I moved here. After a while, you just become one of the locals. It's a small island with some tourism, but mostly, it's quiet.

Just perfect for a bastard like me who isn't fit for love of any kind.

FIVE
eden

"BUT I JUST NEED A ROOM FOR one night."

I hope my voice isn't coming out as whiny as it sounds in my head.

The gray-haired woman smiles sympathetically but shakes her head. "I'm sorry, miss. We're not taking any guests due to the storm."

I look around at the activity around the small inn. "Who are all these people?"

"They're workers, dear. They're getting the place ready for the storm." She lays liver-spotted hands on top of the waist-high front desk. "I'm so sorry I can't help you. But it's our policy to evacuate any guests ahead of the storm. The last of them left earlier this morning."

I want to lay my head on the desk and cry.

I've been up since four a.m. and barely slept at all last night. I'm running on fumes, and my internal bitch-o-meter is ticking up as I stand here. "Okay, well, is there another place here in town?"

"They're closed too." She leans forward as though she's imparting a secret. "You know, dear. I don't know what you're in town for, but you seem like a smart girl, being from New York City and all."

"Hold on. How did you know I was from New York?"

She lifts a shoulder and busies herself with straightening pens in the pen holder. "Small towns have big ears, sweetheart. Anyway, you should get back over that bridge before they close it. I'm sure whatever business you have with Mr. Hanover can wait for the storm to pass."

Great, just great. I'm the talk of the town already? A storm is closing in and the town has nothing better to talk about than the desperate woman from New York?

I glance down at her name tag.

Odette...hmmm. The woman from the coffee shop.

I paste my best smile on my lips. "Ms. Odette. You've got a new grandbaby, don't you?"

Her faded blue eyes light up. "Why, yes I do. Would you like to see some pictures?"

Before I can answer, she pulls out her phone and scrolls to her photo gallery with the adeptness of a fourteen-year-old. "Her name's Maddie."

I smile a little bigger. "She's a beautiful baby."

Odette proceeds to show me a couple of pictures of Maddie, and I make the appropriate noises.

When there's a small hole in the conversation, I push through it. "She's lovely. Now I have a question for you. If, let's say, Maddie were stuck on an island with no place to stay, you'd want someone to help her out, right? Give her shelter?"

Her eyes widen. "Well, yes, of course."

I raise my brows and keep my smile firmly in place. "So, can you help a girl out?"

She smiles again. "I'm sorry, no."

I drop my smile. "I'll pay you a thousand dollars."

The sweet grandma smile disappears. "Nope."

I resist the urge to stomp my foot. With a sigh, I slide my purse off the desk. "Fine. Thanks, Odette."

My tone tells her I'm anything but thankful.

"Safe travels, dear."

Her tone's overly cheery. The woman has the innocent-looking grandma thing down pat. But that little glint in her eye tells me she enjoyed screwing with me.

I roll my eyes and walk out of the inn, pulling the door closed behind me a little harder than necessary. Standing on the front porch, I look around the busy little town, the sea breeze blowing strands of hair across my face.

What the hell am I going to do now? I walk down the couple of steps to the sidewalk and head to my rental. I slide in and start it, blasting the AC to keep my blouse from sticking to me and the sweat from rolling down my ass crack.

Clicking on my email, I find the list Katie sent me of hotels on the mainland just in case I needed it.

I grimace, wanting to kick my own sweaty ass for being overly confident that a) Chase would say yes when I asked and b) the local inns would be happy to take me in.

What happened to small-town hospitality?

Blowing out a breath, I lean back in the seat, thinking over my options.

If Odette is to be believed, I need to get back over the bridge sooner than later. Peering out the large windshield to assess the sky, I notice the clouds are beginning to gather.

Fear skitters down my spine as I realize I'm truly running out of time.

After looking over a couple of the hotels on the list, I call and secure a room in Jacksonville. My room will be ready by four, and I say a prayer to Mother Nature asking if she can hold off her fury for another couple of hours.

A couple of days would be better, but since I'm begging, I can't be choosy.

Now to the next problem.

I still have no idea where the hell Chase lives.

It isn't going to be as easy as looking his address up on Google.

But first I need to change into some clothes that don't make me look like city girl lost.

I frown and look in my rearview mirror.

Odette stands on the front porch taking down hanging plants that are blowing around in the increasing wind.

She may have refused to give me a room, but she's going to help me out somehow.

Squaring my shoulders, I get back out of the vehicle, gather my carry-on bag, and head toward the elderly woman.

Approaching her, I smile. "Hey, there. It's me again. Smart city girl."

She glances over at me, setting a plant on the porch. "What can I help you with, city girl?"

"I wondered if I could use your ladies' room."

She stares at me for a moment, her gaze raking over me from head to toe, then nods once. "That's fine. Help yourself."

"Thanks," I say with a smile.

The bathroom looks like the guest bath of someone's home, complete with potpourri in a dish on the edge of the vanity.

I quickly change into some shorts and a tank top and pull my hair into a ponytail I thread through the back of my baseball cap.

My feet thank me when I slide on a pair of Old Skool Vans, giving them a break from the out-of-place Louboutins.

The image in the small round mirror is not the professional look I envisioned when talking business with Chase. I want to look like I have my shit together and that he doesn't faze me one bit.

He doesn't have to know it's a damn lie, but my work uniform is my armor of sorts. And now, vulnerability trembles under my skin. I blow out a breath. "When in Rome..."

I thank Odette on the way out, but she comes around the front desk and steps in front of me, her arms crossed over her ample chest. "You're not one of those investigative journalist people, are you?"

I tilt my head to the side. "I'm sorry, what?"

She waves a hand in front of her. "You know, one of those journalists looking to dig up a story that's best left alone? Chase is a good boy and he doesn't need—"

Chase is a good boy? He's got these people fooled.

I hold up a hand and shake my head. "No. I assure you, I'm not one of those journalists. I would never do that to Chase."

That much was true. We may not like each other anymore, but I would never dig up his past.

It's better left alone.

I shift my bag on my shoulder. "I've known Chase for years. My business with him is just that. Business. I can promise you I'm not here looking for any type of dirt or story to sell about him."

Odette nods slowly but continues her scrutiny of me. "Okay, I believe you. We had enough of that a few years back when he first moved home. And every so often, we get some city slicker in here that wants to dig for secrets."

She draws in a breath, and I swear even though I tower over her, she looks down at me. "I don't mind city people, mind you. Plenty of them come here in the high season to 'unplug' as they say. But most just end up working by the pool on their laptops and those bud thingees in their ears."

She shakes her head as though it's the most ridiculous notion in the world.

I avert my gaze from hers, hoping the fact that I'm one of those city slickers who works on vacation isn't written in neon across my forehead.

Hell, my whole point in being here is work related. "Um. No, I'm not here to dig up secrets."

"Good." She smiles. "Not that you'd get past that brick wall and security gate he's got at that house of his."

With a shake of her head, she frowns. "I don't know how he doesn't get lonely out there on the far end of the island."

Huh. Now we're getting somewhere.

"I know what you mean," I say, playing along and hoping the next thing I say makes sense. "Especially out there. On the far end of the island."

Maybe she'll be kind enough to tell me which end of the island she means.

"I've never been there, you know, but from the pictures on Google, it's a beautiful place."

She tsks, picking invisible lint off her shirt. "But too much for one guy to ramble around in. Of course, we all thought he might end up with that bartender down at the Red Parrot. But she moved. Turns out it was just a..."—she snaps her fingers—"friends with benefits, I think they call it."

What the hell am I supposed to say to that?

My gut churns, and a feeling that's suspiciously like jealousy wants to spew out. "Right. Okay, well, thanks again for letting me use your ladies' room."

"You're welcome, dear. I hope you make it to the mainland before they close the bridge."

I nod with a smile and leave. I need to get on the road and figure out which end of the island to try first.

Back in my rental, I pull up a map of the island. Even

though I've been here a few times, it's interesting to see it from Google Earth's point of view.

Cape Sands Beach is a twenty-mile-long barrier island, and according to the map, the entire north end of the island is a state park. The lighthouse is right in the middle and the south end of the island is a scattering of private homes.

A smile spreads across my lips.

Thank you, Odette. She'd given me just enough to give me a starting point.

"Found your ass, Hanover."

My ride to the far end of the island is slow but beautiful. There's no racing off to anywhere on the two-lane road that runs parallel to the ocean.

Beach houses, local seaside restaurants, and sand dunes dot the landscape, and my body relaxes in spite of the stress that has me in knots.

Stress in a six-foot-two, unfairly gorgeous, abs for days, male package.

The farther I drive, the less civilization I see. The road becomes a mixture of pavement and gravel in the middle of palm trees and other sorts of tropical vegetation.

It curves right, and about a half mile down, it simply ends with nothing but palm trees and Spanish moss-draped oaks on my right and a crushed-shell driveway on my left.

I roll the window down and poke my head out into the salty, hot air, looking around for something that will give me some sort of indication that there's anything out here at all.

But there's nothing. No address, no mailbox, nothing. The only sounds I hear are a few birds and the crash of waves in the distance.

"Well, if I end up on *Dateline* as a corpse in the middle of nowhere, at least the scenery is nice," I mutter, turning down the unmarked road.

In reality, the town's just a few short miles away, but the feeling that I've left civilization behind is strong.

Chase designed it that way; I'm sure of it.

A few moments later, a white brick wall with a security gate comes into view, and this is no ornamental gate.

It's made to keep people out.

It obscures the view of what's beyond and makes it feel like a gate and security wall were just plopped down in the middle of nowhere.

I stop at the small screen just outside the gate and start to press the talk button when a loud buzz sounds and the gates start to swing open slowly.

A prickle of fear skitters down my spine. It isn't the walking-down-a-dark-street-alone-and-hearing-footsteps-behind-you fear.

No, this fear is more personal. More like, once I cross the threshold of this gate, my life is going to change, and I'm not ready for that.

I blow out a breath and lift my foot off the brake. About one hundred yards in, the driveway becomes brick and forks into two directions.

Something tells me to go left so I follow it, and soon, part of the house comes into view. Most of the front of it is so obscured that it looks as though the vegetation and structure are one.

I park in the circular driveway and get out, scanning the area around me. If Chase wanted off the grid, he succeeded. Short of being on a deserted island in the center of the ocean, it's as secluded as it gets.

At the very least, it feels that way.

I walk toward the back of the house and find it sits on a sloping bluff about fifty feet above the water, giving it an unobscured view of the ocean and endless horizon.

With the looming storm approaching in the distance, the choppy sea and sky are nearly the same deep indigo.

I can only imagine what the views from inside are like. Not that I want to find out. I want to get the begging over with and get the hell out of dodge with my dignity intact.

Preferably before the bridge to the mainland closes.

"Well, I see you found me. And early as always. Guess some things don't change."

I jump, startled by his deep voice out here in the quiet. My heart bangs against my ribs, and I close my eyes to regain some footing.

Straightening my spine, I turn to face him.

"Yes, I found you." I cross my arms over my chest and jut out a hip. "Between Odette and Google, it wasn't hard."

He shakes his head and rolls his eyes. "That woman... We don't need Google as long as we've got Odette."

One side of his mouth lifts in a sardonic smile, and his green eyes rake down my body and back up to my face. "That's a bit casual for a business meeting, don't you think?"

"What about you? With, uh, with..." I gesture to his shirtless torso and try to find words.

His chest gleams with sweat. It's so fucking unfair that even as he ages, he still has abs for days and a sexy-ass V.

My mouth goes as dry as the sawdust on his ball cap.

His smirk deepens. "With no shirt? Yeah, but this is *my* work attire. You, on the other hand..."

Green eyes wander down to my legs. "Well, this would be slumming it for you, wouldn't it, sweetheart?"

I grit my teeth at the endearment that sounds more like a sneer. "Look, you said you'd give me a chance to give you details before you completely shut me down."

"I told you I'd listen but I won't change my mind. I just want you off the island."

"Trust me, pal. I don't even want to be on this island."

He frowns before looking away. I study his profile, the hard line of his jaw.

One might think the broody, grumpy thing would be a complete turnoff.

Not this girl.

Evidently, I'm the sadistic type that enjoys playing with fire and therefore finds his hard lines to be droolworthy.

God, I'm so screwed up.

He sighs and turns to walk away. "Come on. You can give me details while we work. Then I can tell you no without any guilt."

"Guilt, my ass," I mutter under my breath, but follow him.

He stops and does an about-face, causing me to almost run into him. When he reaches out to steady me, gripping my biceps, the breath in my lungs backs up as his gaze meets mine.

He moves in close enough that his manly scent surrounds me.

"When you're done with the details, then you can tell me why you ran."

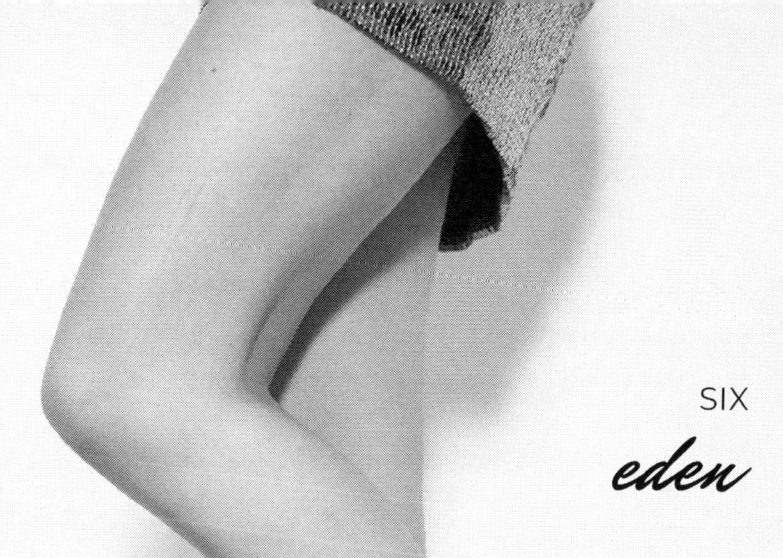

SIX

eden

IS HE FUCKING KIDDING ME?

I narrow my eyes and my voice is tight. "You know damn well why I left. And I didn't run."

"Don't pretend like you didn't get a single message I left you."

"Oh, I got them all right. Including the last one."

His eyes search mine, and it takes everything in me not to let the tears show in my eyes.

After a moment, he releases me, and his eyes glitter with bitterness and a shadow of something else. If I didn't know him any better, I'd say hurt.

But Chase never gets hurt. He only does the hurting.

"I'm not here to rehash the past, Chase. I'm here for business. And if I had another option, I promise you I wouldn't be here at all."

His jaw tightens. "Fine, let's keep it to business."

I glance out toward the horizon and brush a hair out of my face. "Can we go inside at least?"

His smile is anything but kind. "You're not the only one with a business to run, Mitchell. The storm is coming in faster and stronger than predicted, and I've got work to do. You can help."

I scoff at his retreating back. "I don't think so."

He turns and comes back to stand inches from me. "Fine, then why don't you just go ahead and leave before they close the bridge? I'm not going to acquiesce to your request anyway. Get the hell out while you can."

Everything he says makes perfect sense. But there's some part of me that still thinks I can convince him.

It's a gamble for sure.

I can leave, knowing I'm up shit creek with my business and the trip was all for nothing.

I can get stuck here and he still say no and I lose all the way around.

Or I could get stuck here, do my best to convince him, and he agree.

The fact that I still have some hope is the only reason I follow him.

Well, that and the fact sticking around will irritate him.

The palm tree-lined path leads to a single level, craftsman-style home with a detached garage that has its own beautiful view of the Atlantic.

"Get those screws."

"Excuse me?"

With his chin, he gestures to a red box sitting on the ground as he lifts a piece of plywood.

"You know, the little pieces of metal that will go into this plywood to cover the windows? We'll need the drill too."

He carries the wood to one side of the garage, where there are a couple of windows.

Grabbing the items he asked for, I huff out a breath and follow him, trying not to admire the bunch of muscles in his back.

Or the line of sweat that rolls down his spine and stops at the waistband of his jeans.

Even the dark red scar from his surgery that snakes along the back side of his shoulder doesn't detract from the hot working-man picture.

"What do you have in here?" I ask.

"A motorcycle, couple of cars, tools. You know, garage things."

"Are you going to board up the house?"

"Which one?" he asks, leaning the plywood against the side of the garage and picking up the drill.

"Either of them."

"Don't need to."

I look around at the blowing trees and the clouds starting to roll in. "It's been a while since I've been through tropical weather, but I assume they still cause damage."

"The guest house there has automatic hurricane shutters. The main house has hurricane-proof glass. It protects the best, I don't have to do any work, and it looks better. But," he says with a grunt when he lifts the plywood again, "this wood works just fine for the garage here."

I study the structure he calls a garage. It's small, but that is relative compared to the main house. Most people never live in a house the size of his garage, much less his other two houses.

It's a far cry from the tiny dorms in college.

I shake my head. "Whatever you say. So, how am I supposed to help? You look like you got it handled."

"Bring the screws over here. I'm going to lift the wood up, and you're going to drive in the screws about eighteen inches apart. Got it?"

"Yeah, okay, sure."

He hands me the drill, and standing next to him, I line up a screw and drill it in.

It goes sideways though, and even with my limited knowledge of working with power tools and wood, I know that isn't good.

"Eden, you're going to need to get closer to get some leverage on that. Otherwise, none of them will go in straight."

With his head, since his hands are holding the wood, he gestures for me to get closer to him. "Come here. Stand in front of me."

I bite back a sigh and duck under his outstretched arm to stand in front of him. "Like this?"

There's a hesitation and clearing of his throat before he says, "Yep, like that."

The position of our bodies makes me pause.

His body heat is like an inferno at my back, his arms caging me in between him and the wall in front of me.

I bite my lip and lift the drill, holding the screw at the end and trying not to show how affected I am to be so close to him.

With a pull of the trigger, I drive a screw in before moving over the required distance and repeating the process.

"That's it. Just like that," he murmurs near my ear.

His breath tickles the hairs on the back of my neck as we move up one side of the sheet and down the other, our bodies moving together as though we've worked together like this before.

Of course, our bodies moving together has never been our problem.

When I secure enough screws to hold up the rectangle of wood, he drops his arms, but doesn't step back. I lower my arms and briefly close my eyes before turning to face him.

He's close, so close I can see a dusting of sawdust covering his skin and the brown specks that make his green eyes so unique.

The smell of wood, leather, and man assaults my senses and makes me weak in the knees.

I lean against the wall of the garage in order to stay vertical. Even after all this time, all the things we put each other through, he still has this effect on me.

Will I ever get Chase Hanover out of my system?

I have to; I have no choice. As soon as he gives me the answer I need, I'm headed back to New York and my life.

His eyes wander over my face and draw me in, just like they always do.

They're like a tractor beam, and I can't get away even though I know it would be the best thing to do.

"Why is it every time I see you, you're more beautiful than the last?"

He lifts a hand and brushes the back of his knuckles against my cheek. They're warm and a little rough from the dust, but that featherlight touch puts me on high alert.

Warmth spreads in my blood, pooling in my core, causing my panties to dampen with more than just sweat. I sway once, just before I lean my face into his hand.

He shifts slightly and is just inches from my face, his body still so close, but not touching mine.

I wanted to mind it, but I don't.

Our gazes hold, and he brushes a lock of hair away from my face, tucking it behind my ear and under the edge of my baseball cap.

"Am I interrupting?"

Chase drops his head and chuckles. "Fucking Nate."

I let out a breath, thankful for the interruption before I lost my shit and did something I knew I'd regret.

He pushes off the wall and turns toward his friend. "You're making me regret giving you the code to the gate. What do you want now?"

Blowing out a breath, I try to bring my system to rights. There's no way I can get that close to him again.

I need to get him to agree to my proposal and then hightail my ass back to the mainland and on the first plane to New York —and my sanity—tomorrow morning.

"...bridge's closed."

My ears perk up at those last words.

I walk closer to them. "Wait, what did you say?"

Nate turns to me with a smile that almost makes me forget what I was asking. "Hey, you're still here. Good to see you again."

"Hey." I wave awkwardly, a little tongue-tied to be honest with Chase standing there glaring at Nate like he could kill him on the spot. "Good to see you too."

"I see Chase didn't run you off."

I smile. "Nah, he'd have to try harder to do that."

He tilts his head, his smile still in place. "You look like you could hold your own when it comes to Hanover. Fighting back."

Holy hell.

Is Nate Gentry flirting with me?

"That's the best way to handle him."

Chase clears his throat loudly. "Enough, Gentry. You've said what you needed to say so you can head out."

Nate turns to him, a brow raised. "You got a problem with me being friendly to your guest?"

"You're being more than friendly."

"If I didn't know you better, I'd be insulted since I'm a happily married man. I guess since I'm not being a dick to Eden, that means I'm flirting? Don't worry, I think you got the dickhead part covered well enough."

"Move along, Gentry."

I roll my eyes. "Jesus, Chase, leave him alone and quit being such an asshole."

Nate looks back and forth between Chase and me, a grin slowly spreading on his face. "Anyway," he says to Chase, "I hope you got everything you need from the mainland."

Panic grips my throat. "Uh, why is that?"

"We're under a hurricane warning now. We have to shelter in place."

"So that means..."

"The bridge to the mainland is closed."

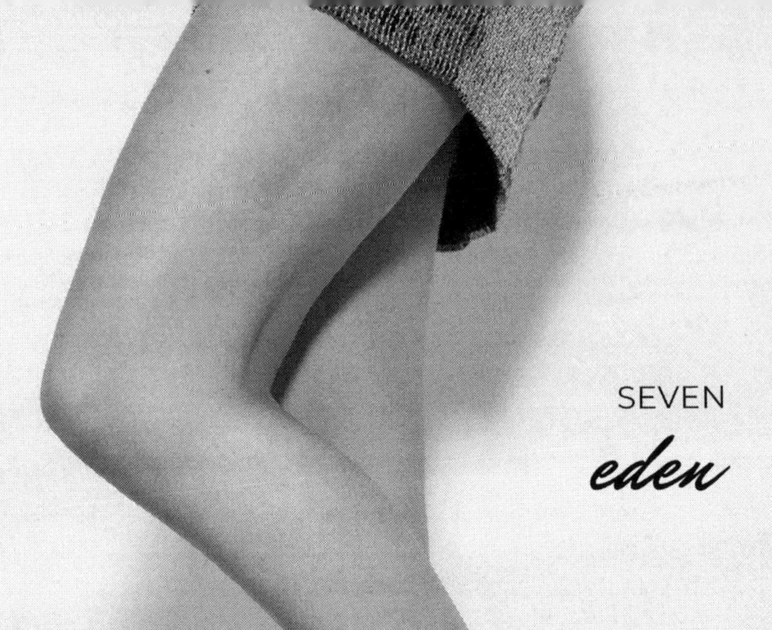

SEVEN
eden

IN LIGHT OF THIS NEWS, I've come to a conclusion.

Karma is not a purring cat for me.

Nope, it's more like a hissing, spitting alley cat.

What the hell am I going to do now?

Not only am I not going to outrun the storm, but I have nowhere to stay.

In a hurricane.

As an event planner, I know better than to think huge events like the charity ball go off without a hitch. But really, who expects their keynote speaker to get hit by a starlet with a drinking problem?

And whose last resort is one of the most popular baseball pitchers in history and just so happens to be my ex-boyfriend-turned-enemy?

Now, I'm stuck on this island with a hurricane bearing down on it with the man who knew every single one of my buttons to push.

Both good and bad.

I really can't make this shit up.

A giggle escapes me before I slap a hand over my mouth.

"Are you okay?" Chase asks.

The two men stare at me like they're wary of my next move and ready to bolt at the first sign of insanity.

Good thing I hide it well.

"Oh, yeah. I'm fine. Just fine." I giggle again and this time I don't try to stop it.

I bend at the waist, my arms wrapped around my middle, and laugh until my sides ache.

The situation isn't even remotely funny. I'm fucked in so many ways. But the thought of that just makes me laugh harder.

"Eden?"

Chase's voice is full of bewilderment, like he expects me to run in circles or start drooling.

I lift up and wipe away a tear that leaked out.

Tears, Eden? Really?

My mother's voice echoes in my head. The woman has always had impeccable timing when it came to making my life hell.

Even if she is six feet under.

"I'm fine, Chase."

"You don't look fine."

The stance of his body is rigid, but his eyes are searching. "And you're doing that laugh you do when you get nervous. Or are about to lose your shit."

"Didn't I just say I was okay?"

Nate clears his throat. "I'm sorry, Eden. But I gotta agree with Chase. You don't look fine, and you're laughing like a loon. I don't know you well, but I'm not sure that's a good thing."

What is it about men when a woman says she's okay and they dispute it?

I look over at the two men standing in front of me and

shake my head.

What the hell do they know about anything in life being hard or unfair?

They are both too sinfully handsome for their own good, with women falling at their feet all the time.

They get paid millions to play a fucking *game* and never have to worry about losing a business due to lack of money.

Okay, that isn't fair.

I don't know much about Nate, other than what I've seen on ESPN. He keeps his private life private.

But my life is unraveling before my eyes, and logic isn't factoring in to my thought process at the moment.

Chase is right, the rat bastard. I *am* about to lose my shit.

I start to pace. "Oh yeah, I'm fine. Just peachy keen. I'm about to lose the business I've worked my ass off to build over the last decade because some young Hollywood star decided it would be fun to drink—underage I might add—and drive her Porsche down the PCH and hit the keynote speaker I had lined up for the biggest event my company has ever hosted."

I gesture toward Chase. "He's the only person I could think of to step in but refuses because I ran out on him after we slept together four years ago after his wife's funeral."

Lifting my arms to the sky, I continue my rant. "Now this storm is making its appearance early, closing off my escape hatch to the mainland where I'd have a bed to sleep in, which is more than I can say for this fucking island!"

My voice ends on a screech, and in the ensuing silence, I freeze and it dawns on me what I just said.

Oh. Fuck.

I drop my arms and stare at the ground, my face warm from the humiliation weighing me down.

Nate clears his throat. "Okay, yeah. I need to head home. Hunker down, guys."

Twigs and tree debris already littering the driveway crunch under Nate's footsteps as he walks away, leaving Chase and me alone with nothing but the wind and regret.

I turn to face him, but keep my gaze on the small expanse of grass between us. Grass that reminds me of his eyes depending on his mood.

"Eden, look at me."

"No, that's okay. I'll pass." I start to turn and stalk away when he catches my hand.

"Eden. Look. At. Me."

I jerk my hand from his because I can't continue to have skin-to-skin contact with him and think straight. But I bring my gaze to meet his. "What?"

Between the bill of his ball cap and the darkening of the sky overhead, it's hard to tell what his eyes are saying.

Damn it. I could always read them before—it's how I knew his moods. In Chase's case, his eyes really are the window to his soul.

Even when his soul is empty.

"I..." He rubs the back of his neck, then lifts his cap and wipes his brow before replacing it on his head. "You don't have a place to stay tonight?"

"Oh, I have a place to stay. In Jacksonville. You know, on the mainland I can't get to."

"Did you check the inns here?"

"Are you serious right now? Of course I did! How do you think I found out about your fortress out here?"

I blow out a breath and try to rein in my temper. As much as I want to blame him for my being stuck here, I can only lay part of it on him.

If he'd let me tell him what I needed from him to begin with, I'd be gone.

And if I hadn't been so arrogant as to think getting on a

plane with a hurricane headed to my destination was a great idea, I'd be outta here.

Or if I'd listened when he told me no and had gone on my way, I'd be on a plane right now back to safety.

God, the *what-if* game sucks.

"I checked both places, and they're closed due to the storm."

My gaze wanders over to the large SUV I rented. It looks pretty sturdy, and surely it has seats that fold down.

Chase follows my gaze. "No way, Eden. There's no way you can stay in a vehicle. With the wind and rain? You're crazy."

My hands land on my hips, and I bring my chin up. "I can take care of myself. And unless you have a better solution, that's what I'll be doing. I'll go park in a parking garage."

It's a completely stupid idea, but what choice do I have?

"There aren't any parking garages around here, Eden."

Before I could blink, he closes the gap between us and stands so close to me, our chests brush. "You are not sleeping in your car. You'll stay with me. End of story."

I fall back a step, my jaw dropping. "With you? Ha, not a chance, buddy."

He rolls his eyes, his frown deepening. "Look, I'm not happy about it either. But it's the easiest and safest thing to do. You're already here."

"Why can't I stay in the guest house?"

"Because it isn't stocked for anyone to be there right now. My house manager is in North Carolina visiting family, and I didn't have her prep it for guests."

One side of his mouth quirks up. "Not to mention, when the power goes out—and it will—you'll be in the dark since it doesn't have a generator yet."

I bite my lip and look out past the house at the dark purple clouds gathering on the horizon. The storm mocks the irrational rage pulsing through my veins.

Not only do I not have a paddle for shit creek, I don't even have a canoe.

At my prolonged silence, Chase tilts his head. "I'm surprised at you, Mitchell. You'd rather sleep in a car than in a huge house with me?"

A smirk curves his lips. "Unless of course, you're afraid you won't be able to keep your hands to yourself."

I scoff, but my skin feels like I sat too long in a tanning bed. "Give me a break. I can resist you just fine, Chase."

"Well, you'd at least have all the creature comforts you're used to in that fancy penthouse of yours. Not to mention, you'd have all kinds of time trying to get me to change my mind about being your speaker."

"I don't live in a fancy penthouse," I mutter under my breath.

God, he infuriates me—thinking he knows me when he has no clue as to who I am anymore.

Well, that and the fact that he still scrambles my brain cells and sets my hormones raging.

I growl and pace away from him. I have to get away from his heat and everything about him that speaks to my baser needs.

Needs that I've been neglecting just like everything else that isn't business related. All hail the vibrator, but it can't replace the weight of a man on me.

My shoulders sag, and I lower my chin to my chest. Damn it all to hell, he's right.

With nothing sturdy like a parking garage around here, there's no way I can stay in my car. It's not only stupid, but it would be uncomfortable.

Only a fool would turn down the offer of a bed in a house

that looks like it can fend off a category five hurricane without breaking a sweat.

I'm sure Chase has outfitted it with everything one would need to hide out for days on an island. Including Internet which I desperately need.

I cross my arms and turn to face him. "Fine. I'll stay here. But only if you put me in the guest room farthest from you. I don't trust you."

He smirks. "Lucky for you, I don't trust you either. I know how you feel about all this." He gestures to his chest.

Warmth spreads through my core and radiates up until my cheeks burn. "Don't flatter yourself, Hanover." I pause, not sure how to proceed without being awkward. "Thank you."

He sighs. "Well, don't thank me just yet."

"Why?"

I don't like where this is going.

"I have guest rooms, but none of them have beds."

My eyes practically fall out of my head. "What? Are you serious? Then how am I going to stay here?"

"You'll stay in my room and I'll sleep on the sofa."

I scoff. "Sleep in your bed? Oh no. I don't think so."

There's no way in hell I'll be able to sleep in his bed among his things.

Everything smelling like him.

No, no, no.

Chase shrugs a broad shoulder. "It's not really a big deal to me, Eden. You're the one making it out to be more than it is."

I put my hands on my head, doing my best not to scream.

Could this really get any worse?

As if answering me—or maybe taunting me—thunder rumbles far in the distance.

Closing my eyes, I take a few deep breaths, trying to think rationally about the situation.

I still need to try and convince Chase to help me. It's my business on the line here. Not just my livelihood, but the livelihood of my employees. Some of them have families that depend on them.

My ego needs to take a back seat. This isn't just about me or for me.

For all of those people depending on me, I can do this. I can be under the same roof as Chase Hanover if that's what it takes to save the business.

"Right," I say, nodding and facing him again. "I need to get a few things. Is there a drugstore or something in town?"

"There's a small pharmacy in town, but it doesn't carry the fancy products I'm sure you're used to."

"Knock it off, Chase. I just need some basic things, like a toothbrush and toothpaste."

And a case of wine to get me through the night.

"Linda keeps that kind of stuff stocked."

"Who's Linda?"

"My house manager. But if you really feel the need to head to the store, there's a grocery store in town. Right off Main Street. We need some food anyway."

He picks up the drill and box of screws and starts toward his truck. I run to catch up with him. "Well, if you give me a list, I'll go get some things."

"No need. I'll go with you."

"I don't need a chaperone, Hanover."

The materials in his hand land with a clang in the bed of his truck before he turns to me. "For God's sake, Eden, I'm aware of that. Are you going to fight me at every turn?"

I look away, unable to meet his exasperated stare. My throat thickens with shame and I swallow hard before I speak. "No."

He gestures overhead. "In case you haven't noticed, we're

up against a time crunch, and it'll go faster if I drive since I know where we need to go."

I don't have to like that he makes a very good point, but I need to concede it.

Think of the business, Eden. That's all that matters.

"Okay, lead the way."

EIGHT
eden

WE RIDE in silence most of the way to town, the tension so thick I can hardly breathe.

If I don't say something soon, I'm going to word vomit something inappropriate.

"As a thank you for letting me stay, I'd like to make you dinner. Have any preferences?"

"I'll eat anything that tastes good."

He glances over at me for a moment before focusing back on the road, a wicked smile lifting one edge of his mouth. "You remember, right?"

I look away, staring out the side window at the passing landscape. "I remember."

As if I can forget.

And it's something I need to get out of my head. Chase has always been an intense guy, and the orgasms he induced were no exception.

When I get back to New York, I need to find a man and get laid properly.

Unfortunately, this sudden case of horniness I seem to be afflicted with has one antidote.

The man sitting mere feet from me in all his shirtless, sexy-as-sin glory.

"Doesn't this thing have air?" I ask, my voice laced with irritation.

"The air *is* on."

I fan my face then reach over to mess with the climate controls. But there are so many it looks like the dashboard of a damn jet. "Well, it's like a sauna in here."

He takes his eyes off the road for a minute to reach over and turn up the fan for my side of the cabin. Cool air blows out, hitting my overheated skin.

"Better?"

"Yes, thank you."

When we come to a stop at one of the few traffic lights on the strip, he looks over at me, a brow raised. "You're planning to drug me with dinner, aren't you? So that I'll say yes to your proposal?"

"Well, hell. You figured me out." I throw my hands up. "Guess I'll have to move to plan B."

"Do I want to know what plan B is?"

I give him a smirk I hope makes him squirm. "Nope. But if we want to make it back to your house any time soon, you'll need to take your foot off the brake." I gesture toward the windshield. "Green light."

He drags his gaze from mine and stomps on the gas, making the truck lurch.

I roll my lips inward to keep from laughing and look out the window until we arrive at the Island Grocery.

The parking lot's packed, and it appears everyone on the island is making their last-minute run for groceries.

Inside, there's a din of noise with all the people milling around, and it smells like a combination of suntan lotion and cleaning products.

I grab the last shopping cart available, and Chase—who finally put a shirt on—heads left as I head right.

"Where are you going?" I ask.

"Beer cooler and meat department. You got the rest, right?"

He starts to walk away, but I block him with the cart. "No, I don't have the rest. You never told me what you wanted. How will I know what to get if I don't know what you want?"

"Surprise me."

Before I can respond, he sidesteps the cart and walks in the opposite direction of where I need to go.

The man knows I need a list; I thrive on them. Gripping the cart handle, I pretend it's Chase's neck.

Infuriating jerk.

I blow out a breath, square my shoulders, and push forward. "You can do this, Eden. You're a professional business owner in New York City. You can handle a single meal with your ex."

The aisles are crowded, the shelves nearly empty, and a fight between two beehived blue-hairs—their hair is literally a silver blue—breaks out in front of a toilet paper end cap.

When the plastic wrap of one of the packages rips and rolls of toilet paper start flying, I take a quick left down the nearest aisle.

And run my cart right into another customer.

"Oh, I'm sorry!"

"It's a mess, isn't it?"

A beautiful, dark-haired woman who looks as out of place as I feel stands across from me.

Her serene smile in the midst of the chaos is comforting. I nod and blow out a breath. "Yeah. It's a nightmare actually."

She chuckles and looks around. "This is the busiest I've ever seen it in here. I tried like hell not to end up here, but"—she shrugs a slim shoulder—"kids always have other plans."

I study her. She looks to be a little younger than I am, dressed casually in shorts and a tank top, flip-flops on her feet, her hair pulled into a ponytail.

But she has a look about her that screams class in spite of the dressed-down attire. She certainly doesn't look like she has kids.

And what, pray tell, are women who have kids supposed to look like, Eden?

When a lull hits the conversation, she holds out her hand. "Charley Gentry."

Nate's wife is a bit younger than I expected. I vaguely recall reading about her in the papers last year.

While she isn't what I expected, she's exactly right for Nate.

I return her handshake. "Eden Mitchell." I shake my head. "I'm sorry. I'm usually better at the small talk."

"First time on the island during a hurricane?"

"During a hurricane, yes. What gave me away?"

She laughs. "The deer in the headlights look was my first clue. I remember the look well. Where I come from, hurricanes aren't a thing."

"Where's home for you?"

She smiles. "A mountain town called Madison Ridge in North Georgia."

I furrow my brow. "How did you meet Nate?"

"Ah, well. That's a story better suited for margaritas and cheese dip. But long story short, his sister is my best friend. He came up for her birthday party and it went from there."

A grin lights up her face. "Meeting him changed all my plans. But I wouldn't have it any other way."

I swallow hard against the ball of emotion in my throat.

Once upon a time, I'm sure my face lit up the same way hers does when I thought about Chase.

Now the only thing that seems to go up where he's concerned is my blood pressure.

"How long have you lived here?" I ask, wanting to hear her story so I don't think so much about mine.

"Well, Nate's been here a few years, but I moved here permanently about a year or so ago."

She tilts her head, her eyes studying me. "Nate told me about meeting you and how you were here to see Chase." One side of her mouth curves up. "Said it was quite the show."

My cheeks warm and I look away, tapping a finger on the cart handle. "I'm a bit embarrassed by that. I don't..."

Charley waved a hand. "I get it. Men can be a pain in the ass. Especially men that look like those two. Add in all that testosterone and the athlete thing?" She sighs. "Well, let's just say I know I'm going to have my hands full the rest of my life."

"Well, hey there."

I look up to see Nate on the other side of the cart.

Just perfect.

"Hey." I wave awkwardly.

"Chase still giving you shit?"

"Absolutely. But he's letting me stay at his house since I'm homeless at the moment."

"Well, that sounds promising. I mean, if he really hated you, he wouldn't do that," Charley says.

"I suppose..."

"Firefly..." Nate rubs the back of his neck. "Leave the poor girl alone."

"Oh hush," she says, patting his arm. "I'm just making conversation, babe."

She winks and Nate rolls his eyes.

"I'm going to get beer," he grumbles before walking off.

Charley giggles and directs her attention back to me. "So, you've known Chase a while? Before he was in the majors?"

"Yeah, we went to college together. But I haven't talked to him in four years."

The thought pains me, and yet I'm the one who'd run and put those walls up.

Looking back, it made sense at the time. It was an emotional time for him and we went too far.

When it comes to Chase though, my good judgment always goes on hiatus.

Her nod is one of understanding. "I get it. It's hard with athletes. I work for the Bull Sharks, so I'm around them all the time. They can be...hard on the heart."

My eyes start to tear up and I clear my throat of the emotions I don't want there. "Yeah, I wish I'd known that a long time ago."

"Fortunately, I love my job, and being married to Nate helps. But I've seen the girls come and go with these players."

"I love my work too," I say, grabbing on to the part of the conversation that has nothing to do with matters of the heart. "I'm actually here for work. I'm hoping Chase will help with an event my company is managing."

"Oh, really? What do you do?"

"I own an event planning and management business in New York."

"No kidding? I'm the manager of marketing and events. What kind of events do you manage?"

"Mostly corporate events. This is a charity fundraiser for a group of businessmen in New York."

"Interesting. Do you only work in New York?"

"Right now, yes. We haven't branched out just yet."

"Well, if you ever need a job, call me. My boss, Darcy, would love you."

"If Chase doesn't help me out, I may have to take you up on that."

I certainly won't be planning any events. The only thing I'll be planning is my imminent move to a cardboard box on the street corner.

There's a pause in conversation as I look at what aisle I'm in. Two thoughts cross my mind at once.

One, I know what I'm going to make for dinner.

And two, Charley may have some info that I really don't need but want.

"What...um..." *Spit it out, Mitchell. You know you want to know.* "Do you know if Chase has a girlfriend?"

She smiles and looks around before leaning forward. "According to Nate, no. There was a girl he hung out with some last year. She was a bartender at The Red Parrot, but moved to Miami about a year ago."

"She just up and left? Why?"

Charley shrugs. "Not everyone here is a lifer. There're three kinds of people that live here. Those that were born here and stay, those that were born here but plan to flee the first chance they get, and the ones that visit and never leave. Tess was born here and was ready to explore. Chase came and never left."

"How do you know it wasn't serious?"

"According to my husband, Chase didn't want it to be serious. Look,"—she leans forward again—"you know him, so you know Chase is a little on the grumpy side, but I'm sure you also know he's got a heart of gold. He's the go-to guy on the island when anyone needs something fixed. And if he can't do it, he hires the best people who can. He helps coach the high school team and a little league team. The kids and coaches adore him, and the town *really* loves him when the team ends up going to state like they did last year. He may have only lived here for a few years or so, but they've embraced him like the prodigal son." She pauses, brow raised. "But then I'm sure you already knew all that."

Actually, I didn't know any of that about him. I open my mouth to ask more questions—questions I really have no business asking—but the man himself walks up.

I clamp my mouth shut.

"Hey, Charley. How's it going? Where's that beautiful baby?"

I can't help it. My head snaps to the man next to me, confusion running riot in my brain.

Who is this man?

Charley grins at Chase. "She's with Julian. Just getting some last-minute supplies. And talking to your friend Eden here."

He frowns, looking down at the items in the cart. "What are you going to make?"

"Hey, you said to surprise you. So that's what I'm going to do."

"Great, *now* you listen to what I say."

He shakes his head and gives Charley his trademark panty-dropping smile that he seems to give everyone but me.

Not that I want it or need it.

"Tell little Lucy I'll be over to kiss her belly when the storm's over."

I might be gawking at this point.

Charley chuckles. "Sure thing. See y'all later."

We say our goodbyes, and when they're out of earshot I say, "Since when did you go around kissing baby bellies?"

He shrugs and stares hard at a can of refried beans, not meeting my stare. "Lucy's adorable. It's hard not to want to give her belly kisses." Clearing his throat, he pulls at the cart. "Come on, let's finish up."

My mind and heart are scrambled as we pick up the rest of the dinner items before making our way to the front of the store, which takes longer with all the people stopping to say hello to Chase.

Watching him interact with the people of the town, I think about how Charley told me he works with the school. Judging by the number of people talking to him, he's a popular guy in town.

Oddly, none of them treat him like a legendary, celebrity baseball player.

The truth is I don't know much about the man Chase Hanover is now. But it doesn't seem to align with the man I once knew.

At the register, the cashier chats like there isn't an odd spring hurricane about to hit, and when it comes time to pay, I hand over my card.

"No way, Mitchell." Chase pushes my hand out of the cashier's reach.

"It's the least I can do." I push back, trying to reach around him and hand the girl my card.

"Put it on my account, please." Chase smiles at the girl, who nods and blushes.

"Yes, Mr. Hanover." She pushes a couple of buttons on the computerized screen, and I swear she has hearts in her eyes.

I roll mine and stuff my card back into my wallet. "You don't play fair, Chase."

"We can agree on that, at least," he replies, putting the bags into the shopping cart.

As we load groceries into the back seat of Chase's truck, Charley and Nate walk by.

"It was nice to meet you, Eden," she calls out. "Maybe once the storm blows over, you can come over for dinner or drinks."

"It was nice to meet you as well. But I'm headed back to New York as soon as they open the bridge."

She nods, but her smile drops a fraction. “Okay, well, maybe next time. Be safe.”

As she starts to walk away, I think of something. “Hey, Charley.”

She stops and looks back. “Yeah?”

“Do you ever miss home?”

Her smile is wistful. “I miss my mom and siblings. But home is wherever Nate and Lucy are now.”

I don’t know what to say to that, but tears spring to my eyes, making me blink hard.

Her smile grows. “Life’s funny, Eden. You just never know where you’re going to end up.”

NINE

chase

AS WE DRIVE down the road, Eden talks a mile a minute.

It's something she always did and I find it fucking adorable.

I don't want her to be adorable.

I don't want her body to call to me like it did when I had her caged against the side of the shed.

I want her to be bitchy, mean, pushy, and the big-city princess I imagined she'd become so I can send her away without thinking twice.

Much to my dismay, she isn't following the plan.

"Did you see those two women fighting over toilet paper? And I'm not talking soccer moms here. These women had canes! I was waiting for bloodshed."

"Yeah, I saw it. They're also best friends except for when it comes to toilet paper, apparently."

Eden laughs, and it hits right in the center of my chest. "Look at that. The island grump made a joke."

"Ha ha."

"Anyway," she continues, looking out the front windshield, "when did you move here?"

"Three years ago."

Right after I blew up my career and hardened my soul.

"Charley mentioned you coach over at the high school. How long have you been doing that?"

"Just the last two seasons. They've got some talent there. I try to help where I can."

"Do you like it here?"

"Yeah, it's peaceful,"—I give her the side-eye—"most of the time."

A smile quirks her lips.

She looks out the side window and silence reigns in the cab. I can practically hear the gears turning in her head.

"Have you made friends here?" she asks, but doesn't look at me.

"Sure. Nate's a good friend, and Ian Sterling, Lucas Raines, and some of the other players on the Bull Sharks. They all live around here. Or on the mainland."

"Hmmm..."

I glance over at her, and judging by the look on her face, there's more she wants to know.

"That's four."

Her head comes around, a quizzical look on her face. "What?"

"That's four questions. You got sixteen more if we're playing twenty questions."

"You're just full of jokes today." She clears her throat and looks away again. "Do you have a girlfriend?"

"No."

"Why not?"

I don't answer, just pull in through the gates of my house, rolling slowly down the driveway.

"Are you going to answer me?"

"Nope."

She lifts her chin. "Why not?"

The defiance in her tone pisses me off, as though I owe her an explanation.

The fact that it pisses me off just shows I give a fuck about what she thinks.

And I really don't want to care.

Parking the truck under the covered part of the driveway, I shove out, slamming the door behind me.

She comes around the truck, ready to talk while I yank groceries out of the back seat.

But I'm done.

Before she can say a word, I round on her, dropping the bags to the ground, barely able to rein in my temper.

"You know why I'm not going to answer you, Eden? Because it's none of your fucking business. You don't get to know how I spend my time or who I spend it with. You made that crystal clear the last time I saw you."

With her hands on her hips, she stares into my eyes and her jaw tightens. The wind blows the strands of hair that escaped her ball cap into her face. "I..." She swallows and tries again. "I'm jealous."

"Jealous? Of what?"

"The woman from the Red Parrot."

My brow furrows. "How do you even know about her?"

She looks at the ground, kicking at it. "Charley and Odette may have mentioned it to me."

I rub my hands over my face.

"Why are those fucking women being a pain in my ass?"

"And here I thought I was the only woman who's a pain in your ass."

I step toward her and she retreats, her back hitting the side of the truck. I cage her in and lean close.

With the wind kicking up around us, her scent surrounds

me like a cocoon. Her eyes soften, desire bright in them. Lips parted, her tongue flicks across her full bottom lip.

That small motion is enough to scramble my circuits.

I want to strip her out of the snug tank top and little denim shorts that are driving me crazy and fuck her against the side of my truck.

There's something about Eden, always has been, that makes me want to possess and protect. I've always thought of her as mine, ever since the first time I saw her.

Part of the guilt I carry regarding my late wife stems from the way I've always felt about Eden.

I never cheated on Heather physically, but mentally, I'd been somewhere else the whole time.

But no matter how badly I want Eden, she's no longer mine to take. I'm not that kind of guy.

And even though I have to keep her at arm's length, I want to drive her a little crazy as well.

Let her see how it feels.

"You're not only a pain in my ass, you make me crazy. You're not just beautiful, you're my every fantasy come true. It's all I can do to keep my hands off you when you're so damn close."

Moving in closer, I lower my voice. "And there's no need to be jealous of another woman. Rest assured, Eden. You're the only one that plagues me."

I glance up to the storm-darkened sky before looking back down into her desire-filled eyes.

My cock hardens painfully behind the zipper of my jeans. If I don't step away soon, I'm going to do something that we'll both regret.

"We're about to get soaked," I say, my voice gruff. I push off the side of the truck and turn away from her before she can reply.

The only sound between us is the howling wind signaling dangerous weather is imminent. We get all the bags inside just in time for the bottom to fall out and sideways rain to commence.

I leave Eden in the kitchen to go check the generator, making sure it's ready for the eventual power outage. With the wind and rain already pounding the island, it's only a matter of time before we lose power.

By the time I get back, she's already put everything away and is gathering the plastic bags into a pile.

She turns to face me, her hands sliding into her back pockets. I sigh inwardly, wishing she wouldn't do that.

All it does is emphasize her breasts, and my willpower is weak right now.

"I wasn't sure where some things went, so I stuck them in the pantry." She shifts her feet and balls up the bags in one hand. "Do you keep these?"

I shake my head. "Usually I keep them for the elementary school to use, but I've got plenty already."

"Elementary school?" Her brows meet her hairline.

The way she says it puts my back up. "Yeah, they use them for projects or recycling where they can collect money." I fold my arms over my chest. "Why?"

"No reason. I'm just curious."

"Well, you don't need to be curious. You're not sticking around."

Her eyes spark with anger, but I have to admire how she banks it quickly, not rising to the bait I toss into the proverbial stormy waters. "Right."

She edges her way out of the kitchen. "I've got to go out and get my suitcase—"

"I'll get it." I head toward the door when her voice stops me.

"I can handle it."

I turn back to her. "I'm aware of that."

She twists the bags in her hands, giving me a narrow glare. "Why are you being nice?"

"I'm not. But it's storming out there, and the last thing I want is for you to be injured so you can sue my ass."

She opens her mouth to say something, but stops and shakes her head.

"Fine." She digs into her purse and tosses me her keys.

I walk out into the storm, sideways rain and wind whipping at me.

But I don't notice it.

I'm too busy trying to stop thinking about anything that remotely makes me want to be nice to her.

Like getting her suitcase during a storm so she doesn't get wet.

The more of a bastard I am to her, the more I'm sure she'll stay away from me.

I'll just have to stay away from the kitchen if she's in there.

My kitchen is big, but being in any enclosed room with her will test any willpower I have with her.

Especially rooms that have a lot of horizontal places.

And I'll try not to think about the fact that her tight, curvy body will be lying in my bed.

A few moments later, I'm a drowned rat with my clothes plastered to me, pulling her soaking wet rolling suitcase.

When I walk into the kitchen, her mouth drops open. "You're soaked."

"No shit, Sherlock."

She's opening drawers, presumably looking for a hand towel, but manages to throw me a look full of daggers.

"Last drawer on the left."

She moves to the drawer I gesture to and grabs a few towels before tossing me a couple.

"Thanks." I pull off my T-shirt and drop it on the floor with a plop.

Out of the corner of my eye, I see her gaze following my hand as I dry off my chest. When our stares meet, a pink blush stains her cheeks, and she looks away quickly, furiously wiping down her suitcase.

I smirk and take my time drying off, adding in a little groan here and there.

When she looks back over at me, I grin and she huffs out a breath, shaking her head.

"Thank you for getting that."

I grunt in lieu of words acknowledging her.

She clears her throat and looks away from me. "Could you show me where I'm staying?"

I rub a hand over my mouth.

When I told Eden—more like demanded, I guess—she was staying with me, I hadn't really thought it through. All I had been thinking about was her sleeping in her rental and the hurricane carrying her car out into the ocean.

Why do I have the feeling that I'm a dead man walking?

I sigh. "Follow me."

We reach for the handle of her suitcase at the same time. She frowns.

"I got it. I don't need your help, Hanover."

"Just trying to be a good host."

"I'm perfectly capable of handling my own luggage, thank you. I did manage not to lose it on my way here."

She puts her hand next to mine on the handle and yanks, trying to dislodge it from my grip.

Some wicked part of me wants to see how far she'll take this idiotic tug-of-war she started.

I yank back, hard.

"Give me my bag," she says between gritted teeth, pulling again.

"Are we seriously playing tug-of-war with your bag right now? I'm not in the mood to play games, Eden."

"Oh, really? Why stop now?"

She shoots, she scores. The woman knows me too well.

My lips curve in a smarmy smile. "Oh, sweetheart. I learned from the best; I'll give you that much."

She lets go of the bag and rubs her forehead, a sigh heavy on her lips. "Fine. Take it."

"You sure? Cause if you want, you can take it."

"Chase." Her voice breaks and, son of a bitch, it guts me. "Please. It's been a long day, and I'm exhausted. I don't care if I sleep on that couch or in the bedroom; just please show me where you want me."

I nearly bite my tongue in half to keep the automatic response of *in my bed underneath me* from spilling out.

That would be a fucking disaster on so many levels.

Instead, I nod and turn away, leading her to the one room in the house she needs to stay the farthest away from.

My bedroom.

At the end of the hallway, I open the double doors that lead into the room.

"This is a beautiful room," she says, walking across to the wall of sliding glass doors looking out over the now stormy Atlantic.

"I like it."

She turns away from the window and glances around the room.

Her spine straightens when her gaze lands on my dresser with some personal items on it and a pair of pajama pants on the end of the bed.

She spins in a slow circle, wringing her hands.

The fact that she's uncomfortable comes off her in waves.

I sigh and shove my hands into my pockets.

Okay, I'll admit my default mode when it comes to Eden is asshole.

But for some reason, seeing her uncomfortable in this situation isn't bringing me the usual fucked-up joy I get by pressing her buttons.

It just makes me feel disgusted with myself.

Her shoulders slump and she rubs her forehead. "I can't take your bed. Seriously, I'll be just fine with the couch."

"Yes, you can take my bed. I've got dibs on the sofa."

It'll make my shoulder hurt like a bitch for days, but I've been through worse.

"Chase, I—"

"How about this? For tonight, you take the bed, okay? If you're still hell-bent on not sleeping there tomorrow, we'll trade. Deal?"

I hold out my hand, which she eyes for a moment, before slipping her slim hand in mine.

Touching her palm to mine is like being shocked. Dangerous and something I should stay away from, but I can't help but want more of it.

"Fine, deal."

Unable to help it, I rub my thumb over the back of her hand, just to feel her skin.

A small gasp escapes her lips, and she lets go of my hand.

Nice work trying to make her feel comfortable, you jerk.

I gesture toward the double doors behind me that lead into the bathroom. "Bathroom's right there and should have everything you need in it. And I'll just leave your suitcase at the door."

She nods, crossing her arms over her chest, hugging

herself. “Thanks for letting me stay. I know it’s the last thing either of us wanted...but I do appreciate it.”

We stare at each other for several beats before I nod once. I swallow the lump in my throat and try to quiet the thoughts running in my head.

“You’re welcome. I’m going to get a few things out of here.”

“Sure.”

While I gather some dry clothes, she sits on the bed and scrolls through her phone, twirling the ends of her hair.

She’s nervous. On one hand, I’m glad because she’s had me on edge since she got here.

On the other hand—the hand that still holds the torch for her—it makes me feel like shit that I’ve made her feel unwelcome.

“I’m going to make a sandwich. Want anything?”

She drops her phone on the bed and stands. “No, thanks. I’ll make dinner tomorrow night if that’s okay. I know it’s early, but I just want to get some sleep.”

“I’ll see you in the morning then.” I turn to leave, but she calls me back.

“Chase, we still need to talk about the speaking engagement.”

Relentless. I bite back a sigh but nod. “I know. Tomorrow. We’ll talk.”

“Thank you.”

“You’re welcome.”

“Night, Chase.”

“Night, Eden.”

TEN

Me: Hey, how are things at the office?

Katie: Eden! Are you okay? I started to worry when I hadn't heard from you.

Me: Well, I'm looking at sideways rain and the thunder is make the windows rattle.

Me: I'm fine given the circumstances.

Katie: Did you make it back to Jacksonville?

Me: No. I'm stuck on the island. They closed the bridge to the mainland before I could get back.

Katie: Oh shit. Were you able to find a room on the island?

Me: Not exactly.

Katie:...

Katie: So where did you stay?

Me: Chase's house.

Katie: *gif of blonde girl looking confused*

Katie: Excuse me? Did I read that right?

Me: If you read "Chase's house," then yes. You read it right.

Katie: Please tell me you have your own bedroom. Far away from him.

Me: Well…sort of…

Katie: I don't know if there's enough money in petty cash to bail you out of jail for killing him.

Katie: Of course, if you use that rat poison I told you about, it's undetectable.

Katie: No body, no crime.

Me: *eyeroll emoji*

Me: You and your crime shows.

Katie: Wait, rewind. What does sort of mean?

Me: It means I have a bedroom, but it's his. The other bedrooms don't have any furniture or anything.

Katie: *gif of woman blinking in disbelief*

Katie: Are you okay?

Me: No, I'm freaking the fuck out.

Me: It's a beautiful room. Would be a nice view of the ocean if it weren't for a hurricane.

Katie: Why do I feel like the hurricane is not your problem?

Me: I'm stuck here and everywhere I look in this room, I see him. I smell him.

Me: And let me be clear, he doesn't stink.

Katie: Eden...

Me: It's fine, Katie. I just need to freak out for a few minutes and get some sleep.

Katie: If you say so. How's it going? Did he agree to be the speaker?

Me: He's thinking about it.

Katie: So he said no?

Me: Anyway, I don't know how long I'm going to be stuck here.

Me: For the moment, we still have power, and Chase says he has a generator. I'll still be able to work.

Me: Tell me how things are going in the office.

Katie: We're all good here. I haven't heard about any hiccups except for when we ran out of Cheetos in the vending machine.

Me: Let me guess, David?

Katie: Yep.

Me: It's a wonder he isn't orange.

Katie: *gif of girl laughing and spitting out water*

Katie: What do you need me to do here?

Me: There's nothing pressing outside of this mess I'm dealing with.

Me: Can you send me the corporate Christmas party file? I need to work on that proposal.

Katie: Consider it done.

Me: Don't worry, I got this covered here. Just hold down the fort there, okay?

Me: I love you forever and when I get home, I'll take you shopping at Bergdorf's.

Katie: I never turn down a trip to Bergdorf's.

Me: This I know well. *smiley face emoji*

Me: Thanks for helping me out. Call or text me if you need anything.

Katie: Will do.

Katie: Hey Eden?

Me: Yeah?

Katie: Be careful, okay?

Me: I'm perfectly safe. I'm telling you, this house is a fort.

Katie: I'm not talking about the storm. We both know this.

Katie: I was there the last time you came back from being around Chase.

Katie: You were devastated. Hell, you both were.

Me: He'd just lost his wife. Of course he was.

Katie: I talked to him, Eden. It wasn't about his wife.

Me: I'm fine. Promise. Thanks for looking out for me, though.

Katie: Okay, boss.

Me: Talk soon.

ELEVEN

chase

I TOSS AND TURN, trying like hell to forget that the woman I'd let waltz out of my life twice is sleeping under my roof.

And in my bed.

While I sleep on the sofa.

Because I'm a gentleman like that.

I turn over, my shoulder protesting like the little whiny ass it is.

Between the hammering all day and it just being fucked-up, I'm in misery.

I finally manage to fall asleep, only to be awakened by the sound of pounding rain and howling wind lashing against the thick, heavy sliding glass doors.

I glance at my phone to see it's a little after six in the morning but looks like the dead of night.

The weather app shows the storm hasn't quite made it to shore yet, meaning conditions on the island are going to get worse before they get better.

We still have power, but I don't expect that to last much longer before the generator will have to kick in.

After using the bathroom, I step into the hallway, and the smells of coffee and breakfast fill my nostrils.

Eden is cooking?

My stomach rumbles, my ham and Swiss sandwich long gone. And as much as I should avoid her, a man's got to eat.

I round the corner to find her standing at the stove, flipping an egg and singing along—terribly off-key—to Bob Marley.

Damn it all to hell, I do not want to be charmed by her or be reminded of days gone by.

But fuck if she doesn't paint an entertaining picture.

I lean against the bar and watch, a smile twitching my lips. She's so lost in the song, she doesn't even know I'm there.

She's been wound tight, trying to make her way in the event planning world in a place like New York City.

I can tell because I know what being wound tight about one's career looks like and how it can suppress anything fun in your life.

Lightness spreads through my chest seeing her loosen up and the Eden I once knew starting to emerge.

My gaze slides from the blonde messy knot on top of her head down to the snug tank top that covers her breasts, to the flat belly that flares into curvy hips.

The curve of her hips is one of my favorite things about Eden. She's all woman, not a stick figure. The flimsy pajama shorts cover her ass but just barely, stopping high on her thighs.

I shift the growing tightness in my pants and bite back a groan.

She turns around, her head bobbing, hips swinging—shit, she needs to stop doing *that* right now—and freezes, her eyes wide as saucers when she sees me.

I smile. "Good morning."

Her eyes dart away, and she reaches for a couple of slices of bread before turning back and moving toward the toaster. "Morning."

"Smells good. Looks like you remember your way around a kitchen."

"Yeah. Want some coffee?"

"Sure, thanks."

"Still take it light?"

I nod. She moves around my kitchen as though she's cooked in it for years. Within moments, she sets a mug of steaming coffee in front of me. I sip and hum in approval.

It's exactly how I like it.

"That's good."

The smile on her face makes her look like she did back in college. "Well, you have good coffee and a rocking coffee maker. Hard to screw it up."

Bacon pops and she moves to tend to it. It smells amazing.

Eden always made incredible meals. But they weren't always appreciated in her house.

I clear my throat.

"When did you start cooking again?"

A pang hits my gut when the smile on her lips is as tight as the little top she wears. She keeps her gaze fixed on the sizzling strips of pork.

"When I moved to New York. I know I said I'd never cook again after everything with my mother. But that was silly. It just wasn't feasible to eat out all the time in the city. Unlike Carrie Bradshaw, I had to actually use my oven."

She glances over at me with a smirk. "I bet you ate out all the time when you lived there."

I shake my head, sipping my coffee. "Not so much. Especially during the season since I didn't have much time. I had a cook though."

"Ah, yes." She points the tongs at me. "So you still didn't have to cook."

I chuckle. "No, I didn't."

She shakes her head and then looks around the kitchen. "I haven't cooked in a kitchen this nice since I left home. The last time, that is."

I study her face, letting her words sink into the silence. "I'm sorry about your mom."

To say those kind words when her mother was such a rotten human is like licking a sweaty jock strap.

Still, it had been her mother.

She half turns to me, her mouth softening a bit. I hold her stare and something passes between us. An understanding of sorts.

"Thanks. She's better off now."

I hear the words she doesn't say.

She's better off now too.

Eden and her mother's relationship had been rocky at best and downright toxic at worst.

Josephine Mitchell had made it her mission in life to make Eden's life miserable just because she could.

Especially when it came to me.

The woman hadn't liked me since the first time she laid eyes on me.

The only thing I've ever been able to figure out is I messed with Josephine's whacked-out plan to keep Eden on a tight, choking leash.

And I made Eden want to break free.

In the end though, the leash had proved to be too strong.

With her chin, Eden gestures toward the living area's floor-to-ceiling windows. "It's gotten worse, I see."

Change of subject. That doesn't surprise me.

I recognize the shuttered emotion in her eyes. It's the same look I see in the mirror every day, and have for the last several years.

"The forecast is calling for it to get worse before it gets better. We're going to take a decent hit from it. I expect the power to go out anytime now."

"You said you have a generator, right?"

I nod, sipping my coffee. "Yep, whole home. You won't miss a beat. Not much of one anyway."

She takes a bite of bacon and nods. "Good."

With a flick of her slim wrist—how long has she had that half-moon tattoo?—the gas flame goes out. "I hope you're ready to eat. I'm hungry and went a little overboard."

She plates the bacon, eggs, and toast, sliding it over to me before plating her own. I lift a brow at the scrambled eggs topped with cheese.

She remembered.

It makes something in my chest pinch, and I don't want that feeling. It keeps me from being pissed off at her.

I scoop up some eggs, letting the mixture of flavors mingle on my tongue before swallowing. "Damn, that's good."

She chuckles. "Thanks."

We eat in silence for a few moments, the noise of the rain and wind and the scrape of forks against the plates the only sounds around us.

We do our best not to look at each other, but I find it nearly impossible to keep my gaze from wandering her way.

It's an odd feeling to know the woman sitting two feet away so intimately and yet not know her at all.

There are two sides to her.

The New York, type A businesswoman dressed in heels that cost more than some people on the island make in a week.

And then there's the casual, laid-back woman in cutoff shorts and flip-flops bought at a drugstore.

Both of them drive me crazy for vastly different reasons.

"So, I guess this wasn't part of your plans for this week, huh?"

She sighs, looking out the windows again. "No. I definitely wasn't expecting to be stuck on an island during a hurricane. Then again,"—she pushes her food around with her fork—"nothing has turned out how I'd planned lately."

Guilt settles in my gut. I've done nothing but put her off since she's shown up on the island, and I know I play a part in her being stuck here. "I have to apologize."

"Apologize?" She tilts her head and takes a bite of her eggs.

I wrap my hand around the fork like I want to strangle it. "Yeah, I feel responsible for you getting stuck here."

Eden chews but doesn't respond for a moment. "It's not your fault entirely. It was my choice not to head back to the mainland. I knew the bridge would get shut down, but I thought I had time."

"Yeah, but I know how tenacious you are, and I could have just let you get out whatever it is you need to get out so you could head back."

Her head tilts from side to side. "Yeah, you could have. But where's the fun in that?"

She's keeping it light and I'm grateful for that. But it still doesn't change the fact that I helped put her in a dangerous situation by letting the old hurts and fears get the best of me.

"I don't know if this will help you or not, but I'm ready to listen."

"Really?"

"Yeah."

"Okay."

She tosses her napkin onto her empty plate and turns on the stool toward me. "My company was hired to manage a charity ball fundraiser, and I've promised them an amazing keynote speaker that would bring in some dollars." She blows out a breath. "I had Mason Jackstone all lined up and ready to go."

I wish Mason Jackstone no ill will, but the man is a tool. He doesn't need to be anywhere near Eden.

My brows draw down. "Didn't he just have a motorcycle accident?"

Her eyes widen. "You heard about it?"

I shrug. "Well, yeah. Everyone did." I smirk. "We might be an island and an isolated one right now, but we do get satellite TV out here. Hell, we can even get Google out in these parts."

She rolls her eyes, rubbing her temples. "Ha, ha. You're a funny guy, Hanover. How did everyone know about this before me?"

"My guess is that you don't watch TMZ."

"My assistant already lectured me on the merits of watching entertainment television when dealing with entertainers."

"That's probably helpful."

"Probably."

"So, now he's out, and you're left with no keynote speaker," I say, pushing my plate away.

"Exactly."

"And you want me to be your new speaker."

She taps a finger on the counter. "Yes."

It's my turn to look out into the storm beyond the windows. Water runs in sideways rivers along the glass, caused by the lashing rain and winds.

"When is the event?" I ask.

"Two weeks from today."

My brows lift. "Two weeks?"

She nods, a sheepish look crossing her face.

Well, shit. I can't be ready for that.

Not only will I have to write some motivating speech to get high rollers to spend their money, but I'll have to be ready to face what I know will be a shit show of paparazzi when they hear I'm back in Manhattan.

There's no way I'll be ready for all that.

I don't want to be ready for all that.

She stares at me for a few moments, waiting for me to have some sort of reaction.

"What are the details?"

"Well, it's being sponsored by Drake Morgan, Graham Easton, and Hudson James. Know any of them?"

I nod, sipping my coffee. "Know all of them actually."

She raises a brow. "Get along with them?"

I grin. "Yeah, I do."

"Oh, good!" She smiles. "They'll probably be happy to have you there."

I hold up a hand. "Slow down, Mitchell. I haven't agreed to this."

"I know, I know. I'm just saying I'm sure they'd be happy about it."

I frown. "What else?"

"You need to give some sort of inspirational speech."

"Obviously."

"Your expenses will be covered and you'll be paid a speaking fee."

She tells me the fee, which is generous but means little to me. I'll only turn around and donate it to something on the island.

"What's the charity for?" I ask.

"Childhood cancer. It's near and dear to their hearts."

I pinch the bridge of my nose. It's one of the few causes that I can really get behind.

Truth be told, I love kids and want my own someday.

I'd been so close to having that dream come true.

But everything changed four years ago.

More like ten years ago when I lost the woman in front of me.

God, this sucks.

I sigh. "So what happens if you don't find a speaker?"

She slides off the stool and gathers our plates and cups. Without another word, she begins cleaning the kitchen, avoiding my stare.

There's more to the story here.

Given our history, it took guts for her to find me and ask me for anything.

And yet she did.

"What are you not telling me, Eden?"

She glances up at me for a moment before focusing back on scrubbing the bacon pan. "What do you mean?"

"What happens if you don't find a speaker?"

Her shoulders slump, and when her gaze meets mine, shadows cross her eyes. "I lose everything."

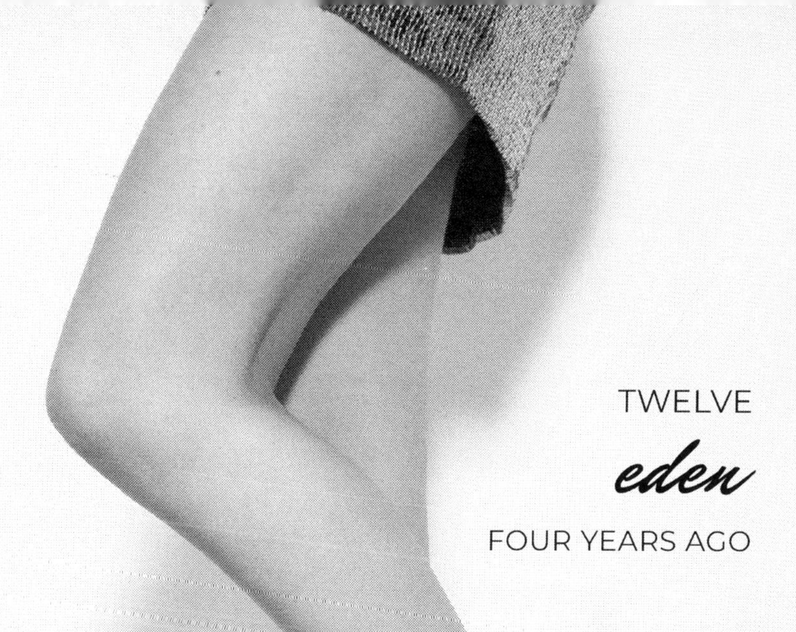

TWELVE
eden
FOUR YEARS AGO

Manhattan

THE SPRAY of bright yellow roses on top of the casket look garishly happy considering the occasion.

Chase stands there alone, his pitching arm in a sling, shoulders slumped, staring at it.

Most of the attendees of the funeral have walked away, sniffling into their tissues, murmuring things like...

"She died way too soon."

"It was a lovely service."

Others, ones I can only guess are Heather's friends, are a little more pointed.

"What's he going to do now?"

"I hear he may get cut from the team."

"I hope the asshole goes to jail."

That one stuns me and makes me want to come out of my hiding place behind a tree and pull the extensions right out of her scalp.

But I let it go.

A couple of men I recognize as his teammates move to surround him. From where I'm hiding out, I can't hear anything they say, but every so often Chase nods his head.

After a few moments, they turn and leave together, the men staying near Chase as they lead him to a blacked-out SUV.

Damn it. I'd wanted to try and talk to Chase. See if he is okay.

I know he isn't, but something in me keeps saying I need to go to him and see how he is doing.

A Town Car waits for me and I give the driver the address to Chase's brownstone on the Upper East Side.

When we get there, groups of people who were at the funeral are walking into his place.

I don't have the courage to go in just yet. So I send the car on and decide to sit in the coffee shop across the street until I do.

Even though it's late in the afternoon, I order a coffee as big as my head to cover the rent on the table I know I'll commandeer for a while.

It's been six years since we've seen each other.

While I want to see him because I care for him, I also want to prove to myself and to him that I've moved on as well as he did.

My leg bounces as I watch the double doors to the building across the street.

Work always calms me down. Too bad I didn't bring my laptop.

Instead, I catch up on emails and texts, keeping an eye on the comings and goings of the people in and out of Chase's house.

Nope, I don't feel like a low-key stalker at all.

After about an hour, a large group of people leave at the same time, including his teammates.

I wait a few more minutes, and when it seems quiet at his house, I head out.

When I ring the doorbell, a middle-aged woman, dressed in Chanel, opens the door. "Can I help you?"

Did I ring the wrong doorbell?

"Uh, hi. Is Chase here?"

Her eyes roam over me before narrowing. "He has no comment."

She starts to close the door, but I put a hand on it to stop it.

No small feat since the door feels like it weighs about two thousand pounds.

"I'm not a reporter. I'm..."

What the hell am I to him now? Saying "his ex" seems like bad form.

"...an old friend. I just wanted to pay my respects. Can you tell him Eden Mitchell is here?"

The woman's whole demeanor changes. She gives me a bright smile and welcomes me. "Eden, oh, please come in."

"Thank you."

Closing the door behind me, she says, "I've heard a lot about you."

She has?

I'm not sure what to say to that.

"I'm Millie, Chase's assistant."

We shake hands. "Nice to meet you, Millie."

"I'll let him know you're here."

She heads off and I take in my surroundings.

Waitstaff bustles around cleaning up glasses and plates that were left behind.

There are long tables full of leftover food, and with my

stomach already in knots, it makes me slightly sick and I turn away.

Oddly, it feels more like the dregs of a dinner party than a funeral wake.

Even still, the townhouse is beautiful, all modern and decorated like it's ready for its close-up at all times.

But there's not a hint of Chase anywhere.

"Eden?"

I turn to find Millie behind me, smiling. "Chase is on the rooftop."

"Oh, okay."

Well, shit. I didn't come here to climb four flights of stairs.

It must be written on my face because Millie grins. "Don't worry, there's an elevator."

"Thank goodness."

A few moments later, the elevator doors swish open to reveal a rooftop terrace bigger than my loft.

I step out and the hairs on the back of my neck rise.

He's looking at me. I can feel his eyes on me.

It's always been like that with him.

Turning to my right, my gaze zeroes in on him standing in the center of the terrace.

The low setting sun casts a golden glow around his perfectly tousled hair, strong jaw, and sculpted bare chest.

Even the jagged red scar doesn't detract from how good he looks to me.

My mouth waters as I take in his abs and the V that leads down into his swim trunks.

And the fact that I'm lusting after this man when his wife is hardly cold in the ground makes me feel like I made a mistake coming here.

He gives me that smile. The smile that once upon a time I foolishly thought was just for me.

Even though I know it isn't true, it still sends the butterflies in my stomach into a tizzy.

"Hey, Eden."

"Hey, Chase."

He opens his arms and as if I'm stuck in a tractor beam, I gravitate to him.

For the first time in six years, I'm in the arms of Chase Hanover.

I feel like I'm home.

His chest is warm, and he smells the same way I remember.

"Eden."

His voice is a soft whisper against my hair, and he holds me tighter.

After a few moments we pull away and I look down. "Where's your sling?"

"How do you know I have a sling?"

"I, uh...I was at the funeral."

His eyes widen. "You were? I didn't see you."

"I was in the back."

"You should have come and said something."

I shook my head. "I didn't feel like it was the right time or place."

He makes a noncommittal sound and looks down at his arm. "I took the sling off. I hate wearing it."

I open my mouth, and he places a finger over my lips with a smile. "I know, I know. I should follow doctor's orders. And I will But I was just about to get into the hot tub."

Glancing over my shoulder, I see steam rising from the large hot tub in the middle of the terrace.

"Oh," I say, turning back to him. "I'm sorry, I'll go. I just wanted to see how you are."

He takes my hands. "No, please stay. It's nice to see a friendly face."

"You just had a bunch of friends here."

He frowns. "With the exception of a couple of my teammates, none of those people know me. Not like you. Want to sit down?"

"Sure."

Taking my hand, he leads me over to the L-shaped couch near a small rooftop bar. Once we settle down with a couple of drinks, he stares at me.

"I can't believe you're here."

I tilt my head and sip my wine. "Why? We're friends, right?"

"Yeah." He clears his throat and looks down. "It's just been a long time."

He meets my eyes again. "But I'm glad you're here."

"Me too. So, how are you, really? I'm so sorry about Heather."

He frowns and takes a long sip of his bourbon. "I'm hanging in there. Truth?"

I nod.

"Heather and I weren't in a good place. And I'm feeling a lot of guilt about that now. With her gone."

"Survivor's guilt?"

"Yeah. I guess so." He leans back with a sigh, stretching his arm across the back of the couch.

I'm sitting on the other end, but his hand is achingly close to me now.

"They tell me I have to meet with the team psychologist weekly as part of my rehab." He scoffs, sipping his drink. "They don't realize the best therapy for me is to just get better and back on the field."

Hearing him say this produces a mix of emotions. On one hand, I'm hurt and angry because I know firsthand how true that statement is for him.

Hell, his decision to leave me had been to play the game.

On the other hand, I hate to see the war of emotions play out on his handsome face. If there was anything I could do to take it all away for him, I would.

But that would require a time machine and different choices.

Essentially, a whole other life.

So I do the only thing I think I can do.

I listen.

And the more wine and bourbon we consume, the more talkative we become.

And the more we stroll down memory lane.

And the closer we get on the couch until we're so close I can feel the heat of his body.

"So, what about you, Eden?" Chase asks, topping off our drinks again.

I've lost count of how many times he's done that, but I don't really care at this point.

All I care about is the fact that I'm sitting here with Chase, and we're laughing and it's like old times.

"What about me?"

"How's life? Seeing anyone?"

"Life is good. My company is growing. It's a lot of work, but I love it. Which means no, I'm not seeing anyone. I'm way too busy for any of that right now."

His fingers toy with the ends of my hair. "Do you ever wonder where we'd be if we were still together?"

Against my better judgment, I lean into his hand and it caresses my face, my gaze meeting his. "Yeah. I do."

"Me too. If I'm honest, I think about you way more than I should." He shifts closer to me, his knuckles brushing across my cheekbone. "I've missed you, Sunshine. So much. And that's not just the bourbon talking."

I close my eyes and inhale sharply, my emotions running riot inside me.

Desire, longing, shame, guilt.

"I've missed you too, Chase. And I can't help it. I wish things had been different."

When the words leave my mouth, I know desire and longing outweigh shame and guilt.

He drops his forehead to mine with a sigh. "Me too. You have no idea how much I wish things were different."

His thumb grazes over my bottom lip. "I've missed this mouth, these lips."

My body is wound so tight that I can barely breathe. I want his mouth on mine so bad, I can hardly stand it.

There's a hesitation about him, as though he's waiting for me to give him permission.

I lift my chin and our lips graze, once, twice...

And then he palms the back of my head and crushes his mouth to mine.

My body melts into him, my hands moving over his shoulders and up into the short hairs at the back of his neck.

He tastes of bourbon, and his mouth alone whips me into a frenzy that makes me feel like I can't get close enough to him.

As one, we move closer together and I arch into him, clinging to him as our kiss becomes more frantic.

He pulls me into his lap and I straddle him, our clothes shoved away until we're skin on skin.

His cock is hard against my slick, wet pussy. I move my hips, teasing my clit with his hard length, making us both breathless.

Those masterful hands move up my back and into my hair, where he holds me close, so close our breath mingles.

With our eyes on each other, I lower down on him, his cock stretching me until I'm fully seated on him.

Our moans mingle, the sounds of the busy city and the real world below us like part of another universe.

We move together like we always did, totally in sync, as though made for each other.

It's as though time stands still. As though the last six years have never happened.

We've never been apart.

Chase shifts us again and I'm under him, wrapping my legs and arms around him as he moves in me.

He slows down the pace, and we go from frantic like we're racing against time to feeling like we have all the time in the world.

But soon, the tension builds and he moves his hips against me faster with each thrust until we're both starving for air.

When we both let go, flying over that cliff into nirvana together, I feel my heart clench, knowing that things have changed between us.

We're in each other's orbits again, and everything I thought I knew before I came here is now changed.

Because now it feels like it's a promise we'll have to keep to each other somehow.

For the rest of the night, we talk, test out the hot tub, and have sex as often as possible.

But it doesn't feel like just sex—it feels like that deep connection we'd always had.

We finally pass out, wrapped up in robes and each other on the couch.

Hours later, as the sun starts to rise, I blink.

And reality sets in.

What the hell have we done?

In the light of day, shame and guilt are the only things I feel.

As quietly and quickly as I can, I move out from under Chase and get dressed.

I scribble a quick note about how nice it was to see him and head out.

Thankfully, downstairs is empty, and no one is privy to my walk of shame.

Well, not until I finally slide into the back seat of a taxi and head home.

I manage to keep it together for the short ride downtown to my apartment.

I manage to keep it together as I take a quick shower, get to my office, and work through a crazy busy day, while actively ignoring my phone.

But that doesn't keep the messages from coming in.

> Hey Sunshine. I missed you leaving this morning. Last night meant a lot to me.

A couple of days later:

> Hey Eden. I hope this is the right number. It's Chase.

A few days after that:

> I know it's the right number now that I've left a voicemail for you and heard your voice.

And his last one:

If you were trying to get even with me for leaving you, consider us even. Have a nice life, Eden.

As much as I wanted to, I don't return his calls or his text messages.

I don't know if that's the right thing to do or not.

The only thing I know is that after the night I spent with Chase, I'm still in love with him and now my heart is broken all over again.

And that's why I can't contact him again.

It isn't until a couple of months later when I turn on the news and his face pops up on the screen when the sports segment starts.

The dam breaks and my tears fall.

And once they start, they don't stop for a week.

THIRTEEN

eden

PRESENT DAY

WHAT CHASE DOESN'T NEED to know is what I really mean is that I'll lose everything I've worked so hard to build trying to forget him.

His brows draw down. "What do you mean you'll lose everything?"

I face him and lean against the counter, twisting a dish towel in my hands.

"If I lose this event, my business will go under."

"But I thought you were doing well. Last time I saw you, business was thriving."

I swallow and look down at my hands wringing the towel.

"I made some...let's call them bad judgment calls over the last year, year and a half. And now I'm strapped for cash. I've had to lay out a lot more money than I anticipated on some things, and I haven't recouped yet. But this event is going to pay enough to take care of some stupid loans I took out that are draining me."

He locks his hands behind his neck and pulls down. "No pressure or anything, right?"

His voice is angry and I don't blame him.

He'd left the New York Admirals under less than ideal circumstances if the media is to be believed.

He and I had one glorious night together that put my heart in danger.

We said things we shouldn't have, did things we shouldn't have, and with my heart broken yet again, I left and never returned his calls.

It's no wonder he isn't exactly thrilled to see me.

For the first time, the enormity of what I'm asking of him sets in, and it isn't fair to put this burden on him for mistakes I've made that he wasn't a part of.

Why didn't it bother me to ask Mason Jackstone to be the speaker? This is business. Would I be so conflicted about this if we didn't share a history?

I shake my head because I don't even need to answer that. All kinds of emotions are involved when it comes to Chase.

Still...I have people depending on me. They have families and lives.

But so does Chase.

What a fucking mess.

He shoves the stool back and walks over to where I stand. "I need to think it over, okay?"

"Fair enough." I pick up the dirty egg pan. "I'll just finish cleaning up."

He shakes his head. "I got it. You cooked; I'll clean."

"No, I can—"

"Eden, leave it."

His large hand covers mine on the handle, and the heat from it sends a shock of desire straight to my core.

I look up into his green eyes that always hold me captive. Honest to God, it was the first thing I noticed when we met in freshman English lit class.

I've known this man for so long and yet over the last several years, I don't know him at all.

Torment mixes with desire in his green depths, and my chest flutters, leaving me breathless.

I need to walk away. Move out of the line of fire before we burn each other again. I don't know how many more close encounters I can take before I combust.

A rumble of thunder outside brings me back to earth and I blink, snatching my hand away. "Fine. I'm just...I've got some work to do so...I'll be...just...yeah."

He nods slowly, his eyes not leaving mine. When they do, he looks down at the pan like he doesn't know how it got there. "Right."

I take a step back and then another before turning and nearly fleeing out of the kitchen.

Moving quickly down the hallway to Chase's room, I'm anxious to be alone so I can recalibrate my body.

I shut the double doors behind me, leaning back on them.

Chest heaving, my eyes slide closed as I drop to the floor, trying to bring equilibrium back to my system.

There's no way I'd survive us coming together and leaving each other again.

The first time I'd felt like I had no good choice. The guilt laid on me by my mother had broken me.

Broke us.

At twenty-two, I still hadn't been strong enough to buck my mother even though I knew what she was doing to me.

She'd been sick at the time, but the woman hated to see anyone happy, including her only daughter.

And she'd used her illness and my inability to say no to her to hold me back when Chase wanted me to go with him when he made the majors.

But at the time, what did I know about a broken heart?

The second time, though?

I knew what a broken heart felt like, specifically a heart broken by Chase Hanover.

I should have known better.

He'd just lost his wife and I'd wanted to comfort him, but we'd taken it a bit too far.

With a heavy sigh, I peel myself off the floor. My pity party for one has officially become pathetic.

It's time to get myself out of personal mode and back into work mode. I may be trapped on the island, cut off from civilization, but it's still a workday.

I put in my earbuds, start a deep focus playlist, and work for several hours, only looking up when the power shuts off, plunging the room into shadows.

Across the room, beyond the windows, the weather conditions have deteriorated. It's becoming hard to see much outside the window from the rain lashing against it. Thunder is an almost continuous roll, and lightning bolts split the purple skies.

Licks of fear scrape along my skin, and I worry about the strength of the glass. Chase says they're hurricane windows, so I assume they'll hold.

God willing.

The ocean churns, dark gray and angry, no longer the navy blue beauty on a clear day. Whitecaps dance along the top of the waves that crash against the shore, and the storm surge marches up the beach.

I swallow hard and pull the curtains closed.

The knock on my door startles me. Butterflies instantly swarm in my belly knowing Chase is on the other side.

When I open the door, he stands on the threshold, hands in the pockets of low- slung jeans and a white T-shirt stretched across his broad shoulders. "Hey. You okay?"

"Yeah, I'm fine."

"The generator should kick on soon. It usually doesn't take long."

I nod and avoid his stare. "That's great. Thank you."

Just then, the room lights up from the lamps I'd had on, and beeps from various electronics go off. The white noise hum of power surrounds us.

"See? Hardly missed a beat," he says.

"Yeah." I tap my finger against the door and shift my feet. When did we become awkward with each other?

When you ran off and didn't speak to him for four years.

Man, I hate awkward.

Chase rocks back on his heels. "I didn't eat lunch, and I noticed you didn't either. Want to share an early dinner?" His gaze holds mine when he says, "We need to talk about some things, Eden."

He's right, no way around it.

In business, I'm good about facing things head-on.

My personal life is another story.

The business of my heart and the business of putting on a good show are two different things.

Even if there is a fine line in there somewhere.

I straighten my shoulders and nod. "Sure. I owe you dinner anyway."

He shakes his head with a sweet smile that for a moment reminds me of the little boy I'd grown up with. "Consider breakfast payment. I got dinner. I'll see you in the kitchen."

"Deal. I'll be there in a few minutes."

A quick change into a pair of well-worn jeans and a tank top and I head toward the kitchen, where I find Chase slicing up a slab of red meat.

He nods toward the bottle of my favorite beer on the

counter. "I don't know if you still drink that or not, but I took my chances."

"Thanks." I squeeze the lime in the top and take a long sip.

My insides sigh when the icy cold carbonation hits my tongue. I swallow the smooth liquid, letting it warm me from the inside out. "You remembered."

His gaze lifts to mine, a swirl of emotions in his green depths. "I remember everything."

After a beat, he goes back to slicing the meat, and I stand there tongue-tied and on the verge of tears, unable to do much more than stare at him.

"It looks like you were going to make fajitas."

"I was." I groan and put a hand over my empty, and now growling, belly. "I was going to try and copy your steak fajitas. But I doubt I would have made them as good."

He grins. "Still your favorite?"

"Hell, yeah."

Because not only is the man a legendary baseball player who looks like an Adonis and made me see stars in bed, but he can also cook that fine baseball ass off.

Especially fajitas.

I prop an elbow on the counter and drop my chin into my hand. "What seasoning do you use to make it taste so good? I've tried different brands and can never find one as good."

He shakes his head as he slides the meat off the cutting board and into a bowl. "Can't tell you that. Family recipe."

"What do you mean by a family recipe?"

A smile touches his lips as he works. "The foster family my mother lived with when she was a teenager had a grandmother that would come over, and she was Mexican. Had a special recipe she used that my mother remembered. And she taught us."

"Really? I didn't know your mom was in the foster system. You never mentioned it."

He reaches for a green pepper and starts to chop it with precise movements. "It's not exactly a topic of conversation I talked about with people. I wasn't ashamed. It just never came up."

"Yeah, but..." I trail off, sipping my beer.

We'd been more than a passing boyfriend, girlfriend thing. We'd made future plans, confessed our love. And I still didn't know.

He shrugs a shoulder as he scrapes the peppers off into the bowl with the meat. "It's not a big deal, Eden. She didn't really talk about it with us. I guarantee that most of the women at her supper club never knew either."

Silence surrounds us, leaving only the sound of the knife blade hitting the cutting board.

Outside, the wind continues to howl and the rain keeps beating against the house.

In spite of the fit Mother Nature pitches beyond the windows, a relaxed sort of peacefulness settles in my bones as I watch him work.

Then again, up until ten years ago, Chase had always been my safe space.

It's no mystery why my heart has had a void in it since the day he left for the majors.

I'm sure my therapist would tell me the fact that I'm in his house that's built like Fort Knox against the elements during a hurricane isn't a mistake.

"Anything I can help with?"

"No, I've got it under control. Just enjoy your beer."

I slide onto a barstool and lean back, letting my shoulders relax after working in a less than ergonomically friendly position. "I won't say no to that."

As I watch Chase assemble dinner, I think back with a smile to the few times he'd cooked for me before. "You know, this isn't the first time you've cooked for me on this island."

He looks over at me with a smile, stirring the spicy mix of meat and veggies. "I remember. When we came over here for the day on spring break and pitched a tent on the beach. These are better surroundings though."

I laugh. "No doubt. Although, I admit camping on the beach was pretty romantic. Until we got caught."

"The guy who busted us just retired from the sheriff's department here last year."

"Seriously? Did he remember you?"

"Unfortunately."

"Oh no," I say, laughing.

"He was cool about it. You know, gave me that elbow nudge, wink thing." He mimics the motion, which makes me laugh harder.

"Oh, that's classic." I sip my beer. "I will say though, this food smells better than what you cooked back then."

He lays a hand over his heart in mock hurt. "You mean, you didn't enjoy my grilled mystery meat on a stick?"

I wrinkle my nose. "Yuck. Well, I'm lying. I did enjoy it back then. But I think our palates are a little more refined these days."

"Definitely," he says with a grin. "At least, in some areas."

His eyes are full of heat and make my skin flush. I don't know what to make of that comment or the look he's giving me.

Or the change in his attitude toward me.

I narrow my eyes at him. "Why are you being so nice to me? Where's Chasey McGrumpypants?"

He stops midstir and turns to me. "Did you just call me Chasey McGrumpypants?"

"That's my new nickname for you."

"You make me sound like a Sesame Street character," he grumbles.

I point at him. "Hey, it sounds like he's coming back. Whew." I mimic wiping sweat from my brow. "I thought I'd lost him there for a minute."

He rolls his eyes and lowers the heat under the pan before turning to me. "It's like you said. This isn't the scenario either of us wanted, but it's what we have. There's no reason to make this any harder than it has to be. I'm trying. Okay?"

His eyes are sincere, even if those full lips are frowning.

"Okay."

I can't tear my eyes from his mouth. My mind wanders down memory lane to our camping trip on the beach.

It had been romantic, but he'd said and done some seriously dirty things with that mouth underneath the stars with the waves as our soundtrack.

The memories play like a film reel in my mind, and I have to clench my thighs together to ease the hurts-so-good pain between my legs.

His gaze hasn't left mine, and it's gone from sincere to sexy the longer we look at each other.

The food isn't the only thing sizzling in this kitchen.

I need to break this eye fucking before I lose it.

"I'll get the plates and silverware ready," I blurt out, jumping off the stool.

He nods and turns away to stir the food. "It's just about ready."

We work together in the kitchen, moving around each other like a dance and yet giving each other enough space that we never get too close.

If I get too close to him for too long, I'll strip down to my birthday suit and beg him to fuck me on the granite countertops until I forget why I'm here in the first place.

With steaming plates full of food and our beers, we move into the informal dining room.

I call it that in my head because the table is much smaller—though it still could seat six grown men with elbow room to spare—than the monstrosity of a table in the separate room off the kitchen.

I'm starving and without thinking about it, I start filling my face with fajitas.

"Oh my God," I say around a hot bite of food. "This is amazing." I put my hand over my mouth and swallow. "I'm sorry, that was rude."

"It's nice to see you loosen up a bit, Mitchell." Chase chuckles and opens another beer for each of us.

I make a mental note to drink this one a bit slower. I need to be somewhat sober around this man.

"What do you mean? I know how to loosen up."

He chews and swallows before speaking like a well-mannered adult. "Oh yeah, of course you do."

"You don't know me as well as you think you do."

"What do you do on a Saturday night?"

"Like a regular Saturday night or something special?"

"A regular, run-of-the-mill Saturday night."

I think back over the past few months. I can't remember the last time I went out for drinks with my friends.

And the last time I did, my phone was glued to my palm. I have no idea what is going on with their lives.

I blink and then huff. "I'm running a business, Chase. Who has time for recreation?"

"Is that what you're calling sex now?"

The blush burns my cheeks. "No. I...no," I stammer.

"I'm running a business too, Eden. But I still find time for... recreation."

I lift my bottle to drink away the jealousy that burns in my throat. "Yeah, I know. We already talked about that."

Jealousy isn't a pretty thing and an emotion I need to check at the door when it comes to Chase. But right now I'm epically failing at that.

And here I thought I'd gotten over it when he got married.

But who could blame me?

The man is straight-up gorgeous with all that chocolate-brown hair and those green eyes. He'd had groupies hanging around the dugout, even back in college. I'd trusted him back then because he'd made it clear I was it for him.

But trust is a high-dollar commodity that is easy to lose and hard to win. It was a difficult lesson I'd had to learn.

Great, now I'm all awkward again and feel like I'm about six years old pushing my food around my plate.

I straighten my shoulders and clear my throat. "You said we needed to talk. What did you want to talk about?"

There. Steering the conversation back to more professional topics is just the antidote to my plague.

The wind, rain, and thunder batter the house from the outside. But the way he blows out a breath before meeting my gaze gives me the feeling I'm going to be battered here on the inside.

"I can't be the speaker for your fundraiser."

In spite of the fact I'd been expecting this answer, my dinner threatens to make an encore appearance.

He rubs a hand over his stubbled chin, looking a little sick himself.

"I know how much this means to you, Eden. I really do. But I need you to understand why I can't go back to New York right now."

I want to kick and scream and cry.

But there's something in his tone, a shadow that crosses those green eyes, and the tightening of his jaw that makes me sit up and take notice.

I push aside the panic building in my chest and nod. "Please tell me. Because right now, I gotta be honest. I need something to keep me from spinning out of control."

Chase pushes his plate aside and leans back in his chair, arms crossing over his chest. The sleeves of his T-shirt pull tight over his biceps, the muscles in his forearms on full display.

For long moments, he sits staring into space, but it isn't a vacant stare. It's one of a man reliving a period of time he'd rather forget but knowing he never can.

Once upon a time, I could read the man like a book. Instinctively, I know whatever it is that made him a closed book now has to do with the death of his wife and career.

My gut also tells me there's more to the story than a tragic car accident that ended with her dead.

"I don't even know where to start."

"How about from the beginning?"

He blows out a breath and nods once, looking as though he's mentally taking a step off a cliff. "You know about the car accident."

"I think the whole world knows about the car accident. And your subsequent release from your contract."

A muscle in his cheek tics as he holds my gaze. "Yeah, what they don't know is the truth."

FOURTEEN
chase

EDEN'S EYES widen at my statement.

She and I don't owe each other anything, but I care for Eden—far more than I should—and she deserves to know why I can't help her with such a big favor.

My hands clench into fists. "Remember when I told you things between Heather and me weren't good?"

"Yeah, you just never went into it."

I meet her eyes. "Yeah, we didn't talk too much after that."

Our gaze holds for a moment before I look away. "Anyway, at the time I wasn't ready to talk about it. Especially with all bullshit the PR for the team was spewing. It was for the great All-American image the clubhouse wanted me to portray. I mean, I played America's game. My wife was a former beauty queen."

Pausing, I raise my gaze to Eden, who's staring down at her bottle. "Anyway, we weren't happy. Heather was..."

How does one speak ill of the dead? Even if it's the truth? I'm going straight to hell for what I'm about to say, but I'm being honest. "Heather was a demanding, spiteful bitch."

Eden's jaw drops. "Wow. That isn't at all how any of that came across."

I nod my head once. "Yeah, the PR department for the clubhouse certainly earns their salary."

"I guess so."

"Anyway, things weren't great. I wanted a divorce, but stupidly I didn't have a prenup—"

"Wha—"

"Don't ask. Anyway, I knew she'd try to take me to the cleaners. So I had to play my cards carefully."

I look down at my hands, slowly uncurling them.

Once upon a time, my right hand held a baseball like it was an extension of my arm. But it would never hold a ball in quite the same way again.

Sighing, I continue. "Then she told me she was pregnant. I was happy and yet I also felt...trapped. And I can remember thinking to myself that it seemed odd since by this point, we hadn't been sleeping together much anymore. But there had been one random night..."

Eden clears her throat and shifts in her seat. I glance up and grimace.

Her lips are pursed together as though she's tasted something sour. I can't say I blame her.

If she started talking about any of the guys she'd been with since me, I'd lose my shit, no doubt about it.

Hypocrite much, Hanover?

"The point is, I knew I couldn't divorce her yet. I mean, she was about to have my child. She said she was about two months along. I went with her to the doctor's appointment, heard the heartbeat, and..."

I clear the emotion from my throat. "I knew without a doubt I had to try and make it work for the sake of the tiny peanut on the screen whose heartbeat raced in my ears."

The ultrasound is something I'd filed away deep in the recesses of my brain. After everything that happened, it was just too much to think about. "I need more beer. Want one?"

She nods and stands as well, picking up our plates. "How about we get this cleaned up before you continue?"

It's as though she senses that what comes next will be hard.

She doesn't know the half of it.

I'd never told a soul what I'm about to tell her.

The strange thing is, I trust Eden implicitly, despite our rocky past.

We clean up the dishes and kitchen in silence. But I need to hurry up and get this off my chest before I slide all the way back to that dark place I'd been in right after the accident.

I grab the last two bottles of beer, and in silent accord, we head into the living room.

In spite of one wall of the room overlooking the yard and the ocean beyond it, the large, open room is dim as the storm rages outside.

To save energy, we light a few candles instead of turning on the lights. They cast a warm glow in the room, throwing shadows of the flames on the walls around us.

Eden sits on one end of the sofa, tucking those long legs up underneath her. I set the bottles on the coffee table and sit at the opposite end from her.

"So, you heard your baby's heartbeat," she says.

I nod, my elbows on my knees, both hands tucked under my chin. "About two weeks later, we went to dinner. I'd been on a long road trip, one of the longest stretches since we got married, and we hadn't talked much either. Kept missing each other on the phone. She said she had something she wanted to talk about."

Rubbing my damp palms up and down my thighs, I do my best to keep the combination of residual guilt and anger at bay.

"Heather was out at the Hamptons house. I had the car service take me out to the house from LaGuardia, since I didn't keep my car in the city. We went into the village, had a nice dinner, at least for a little while. Then she started in on me about being gone so much, but what the hell was I supposed to do?"

Try as I might, I can't seem to stop the tangents of frustration that come out.

"It's my job, for Christ's sake. And God knows she loved the lifestyle my job brought her."

Bitterness tastes like metal on my tongue, and I hate that it's still there.

I glance over at Eden to find her watching me quietly but with no judgment in her eyes.

She lowers her chin as though to say "go on" but never verbally pushes.

"Anyway, I ended up drinking too much, and she'd still never gotten to her point. I decided it was better for her to drive us home. She threw a fit because she hated driving, but there was no way I was leaving my Ferrari there in town."

I shake my head, a humorless smile on my lips. How different life would have turned out if I'd just left the car there.

"It was the worst decision I could've made. Heather ended up driving us home, and we argued. She was so angry with me for a number of things. Drinking too much that night, being gone...you name it, she was pissed about it. And that's when she told me."

I blow out a breath, willing my dinner to stay down and my stomach to stop tumbling.

"Turns out, she never loved me and wanted a divorce.

She'd starting seeing someone else two months after we got married and continued to see him for the entire two years of our marriage."

Realization dawns in Eden's eyes and she gasps softly. "Oh no. Chase, don't tell me..."

"The kid wasn't mine. It was the guy she'd been fucking around with behind my back."

She closes her eyes but doesn't say anything, thankfully. I can't tolerate pity. I'd seen enough of it after Heather died.

"Long story short, we started yelling at each other. And I asked her..." I swallow against the lump in my throat. "I asked her who the poor fucker was that she'd suckered into her web of lies. She looked over at me, took her eyes off the road, and told me who it was just as a flash of something caught my eye in front of the car. All I remember is yelling at her to watch out and then we were spinning. After that, I woke up in a tangle of metal."

My vision goes hazy and I'm back on that dark road, the smell of earth mixed with gasoline, smoke, and blood all around me.

"I looked over at Heather and saw that she was...dead. Her side of the car had taken the brunt of force when we hit the tree. I kept passing out and waking up. My arm was bleeding. I felt it, but I couldn't move to see how bad it was. The last time I passed out and woke up, I was being lifted into an ambulance."

I rub my bicep over my T-shirt, brushing over the scars. "I had surgery on my shoulder, and they put some pins in it. The next day I woke up, and the police came in to get the story of what happened, what I could remember. I never told them about our argument. I just told them that Heather swerved to miss a deer and we hit a tree. And they confirmed she and the baby died at the scene."

I fist my hand again, regret coursing through me, but when I hear a sniffle, I turn my head.

My heart hurts to see tears coursing down Eden's face.

When our eyes meet, she wipes them away. "Chase, I had no idea. I'm so sorry."

"Thanks. But it was my fault. The accident."

Her eyes widen. "How can you say that?" Her voice pitches higher with every word she says.

"Because it's the truth, Eden. My wife and a child who never had a chance at life are dead because of me."

Her lips turn down into a frown. "Chase, that's ridiculous. You weren't even driving."

My skin crawls, and I shoot up off the couch, crossing the room to the windows.

The storm outside matches the chaos in my head.

I turn back to her, hands on my hips. Anger runs hot in my veins, and the only place I have to channel it is to the woman sitting across the room from me.

The woman who, no matter how hard I try, never seems to leave my thoughts for very long. Even when I was married to another woman.

"I made a selfish decision. I chose a car over my wife. I might not have loved her the way a wife deserves to be loved, but she was still my wife. And the last words I said to her were full of hate."

Eden rises and crosses the room to stand in front of me. "Chase, it's normal to feel guilty in cases like this."

"Yeah, I know. Survivor guilt and all that shit." My voice was full of disdain. "Spare me the psychobabble, Eden. Been there, done that. During the year I recovered from the injury, the team made me go see a therapist. I had to be cleared to play again."

She looks away for a moment before bringing her gaze back to mine. "You can't keep blaming yourself for it, Chase. You didn't kill Heather and you didn't kill her baby."

"Well, how about this to add to my guilt? If I hadn't been such a selfish prick, my baseball career wouldn't be over. How's that for mourning your wife? That I mourned my career more than I did her?"

By the time I say the last word, I'm shouting.

"How long were you and Heather together?"

I blink. "In total, three years."

"And how long have you been playing baseball?"

"Nearly my whole life. I started in T-Ball. You know that."

"Exactly. Baseball has been your whole life. It's understandable that you mourn it. You lost a vital piece of your life, Chase. And anyone who says different is a liar."

Losing baseball had been like losing a limb, not just injuring it. Baseball was a part of me I was so comfortable with, I knew every move.

Until I didn't.

My chest heaves with the pain of losing my livelihood—still there even four years later.

But Eden's logic loosens the giant chronic knot in my stomach just a little bit.

I hadn't loved Heather, and she'd fucked me over, but her parents and family had loved her. She'd been someone's daughter and sister.

I'd wanted out of my marriage, but that hadn't been the way I wanted it.

But I hadn't been driving the car either, had I?

Why does it sound so different coming from Eden than it had from all the shrinks I'd seen after the accident?

I've never told anyone how I felt, not even the shrinks, but they knew. They're paid to know these things. Still, it didn't quite sink in like it did coming from Eden.

I swallow hard and turn back to the storm. There's something comforting in watching it rage.

To hear Eden say it wasn't my fault is like she'd found and rescued me after being lost, tumbling around in the dark.

There's more to tell and I'm exhausted just thinking about it. But at this point, I feel the need to tell her all of it.

I sigh and rub the back of my neck, facing her again. "There's more."

Eden's stare is steady on me. "Does this have anything to do with you fighting with Ty Richardson?"

Fuck, this woman is smart.

I frown. "You saw that, huh?"

Her lips curve in a half smile. "Hard not to when it's splashed all over the Internet and TV."

I lift a brow. "I thought you didn't watch entertainment news."

"You made the nightly news, Chase."

I wince and my frown deepens.

"Heather had been seeing Ty Richardson behind my back the whole time. And it was his baby."

Her eyes widen. "That's who she was cheating with?"

"Yep."

"Why would he do that?"

"The guy has had it out for me ever since I set foot in the clubhouse. He thought I had taken his spot on the roster, and he was on his way out."

"Yeah, well, he was. He'd lost his mojo. He couldn't hit the broad side of a barn. I never could figure out why they kept him."

"He was a decent backup. But he didn't want to be backup. It was a cut in pay and a blow to his ego." I shrug. "I guess he figured since he couldn't one-up me on the field, he'd do it off the field."

"That's why you guys were fighting on TV."

"He'd run his mouth to me and about me one too many times, and I lost my shit. It was the last straw. I was still a starter, but my pitching was for shit and we all knew it. That only served to piss him off, and he needled me about the fact that I couldn't throw a strike anymore."

I breathe deep, trying to relieve some of the pressure in my chest. "In the end, he got what he wanted. I threw the first punch and with the way it was filmed, it looks like I hit him unprovoked. I ended up reinjuring my arm, and I was deemed nothing more than a liability to the team. Both physically and for team morale. I was benched for my next game, and a week later, I went in and asked to be let out of my contract."

She shakes her head, her forehead crinkled in confusion. "Why would you do that? Baseball was your life. Didn't you only have another half season or so left on your contract?"

"For someone who wouldn't return my calls, you sure know a lot about me."

A pink blush stains her cheeks, and she rolls her lips inward. "I watch the news."

"Right," I say with a smirk. "You watch sports?"

"Uh, yeah."

"Bullshit, Mitchell."

"Okay, fine. I don't watch sports, but I did watch sports news when you were involved, okay? Happy now?" She huffs, the motion lifting and lowering her chest in such a way I'm momentarily distracted.

I don't known a damn thing about her in the years we've been apart, but she knows all about my demise. And now she has the real sordid details.

"To answer your question though—yes, I only had six

months. Which made it easier to get out of my contract. It was a mutual decision. I couldn't win a game if my life depended on it. The media spun the video and the story so that I ended up looking like the bad guy. Even if I'd wanted to play for another team, no one would touch me. My reputation as the Hollywood Golden Boy was shot to hell."

I turn my head toward the window. "I shouldn't have gone back after the accident. I had all sorts of setbacks with the rehab and then with all the shit that went down with Ty...I was fucked in the brain and that was a bigger problem than the team doctor could crack. After everything that happened, it was easier for me just to get out and move on. Get out from under all the media scrutiny and the lies and just be able to breathe."

"These last few years have been shitty for you. I'm so sorry, Chase."

"For which part of it?"

"All of it. For losing your wife, for being betrayed by not only the woman who was supposed to love you but also by your teammate. For losing the one thing in this world that meant the most to you."

There's a pang in my chest as I look down into her eyes, eyes that hold unshed tears, making them gleam like turquoise gems in the dimly lit room.

Shifting closer to her, our bodies brush together. "You're right. I did lose the most important thing in the world to me. But I didn't lose it on that night."

Her eyes meet mine and there's a swirl of emotions in them.

Hope, fear, desire, hurt, surprise.

"What do you mean?"

I cup her face in my hands. My thumbs stroke the soft skin

of her cheekbones, her eyes sliding closed for a brief moment before opening again.

God, she's beautiful. Stunning.

And it's more than just her physical looks. She stuns me with her understanding and lack of judgment when that's all I ever saw in the months after the accident.

Why did I ever let her go?

"I mean you, Eden."

FIFTEEN
eden

I'VE DREAMED of this very scenario more times than I care to count.

The day when Chase tells me how much he missed me.

That he was stupid for letting me go all those years ago.

He'd profess his love, sweep me off my feet, and give me mind-blowing, toe-curling orgasms forever and ever, amen.

Instead, I'm tongue-tied and frozen to the spot.

Chase leans in closer, his rough, calloused hands cupping my face, his breath hot against my lips.

My heart beats against my ribs in anticipation of his kiss that always weakened my knees.

His gaze is intense and full of emotions.

There's a war inside him, one he fights alone. Every damn day.

It's the burden of surviving something he thinks he had the power to change.

I want to help him lighten the load, but he's still too deep in that guilt for me to reach him.

His gaze flicks down to my lips before he steps away. The

warmth of his hands disappears when he drops them to his sides.

"I'm sorry. I shouldn't have..."

He stops and I can see him trying to collect his thoughts.

And when he does, anger sparks from his whole being, making his voice hard and unyielding.

I can't tell if his anger is with me or not.

"Once upon a time I'd jump for a chance at something like your charity event. Anything for that limelight. But now?" He shakes his head. "I can't face it now. I can't put myself out there for you or for the paparazzi to tear me apart again. I won't let them put this town in the spotlight, either. These are good people here. I won't subject them to that again."

Panic and hurt seep into my bones, but I grab on to the one thing I know I could promise him. "Listen, I can't help what happens here, but I'll have extra security, whatever you need to keep the vultures away from you."

His sigh is deep and laced with swear words he mutters under his breath. "I'm sorry. I just can't, Eden."

Pain slices across his face, and now I see clearly that this is torture for him.

I didn't realize when I came here that the extent of my favor would be so traumatic for him.

But now that I know, how can I ask him to go back to the city where the memories are so painful he can't recall the good ones?

God, I'm a shitty person.

It isn't his fault I'd fucked up. I can't ask him to step back into the fray just to save my ass.

And yet the claw of anxiety and fear in my throat insists I still try to convince him.

What is wrong with me?

The lines of what I want and what I need are starting to blur, leaving me confused as hell.

But I'm not heartless and as much as I pretend to hate him, if seeing him again has taught me anything, it's that I never stopped loving him.

I know what I need to do.

I slide my hands into the back pockets of my jeans and blow out a slow breath.

"You know what? This is wrong of me. Now that I know everything, I can't in good conscience ask you to do something like this." I sigh with a smile, even though panic is now my new best friend. "I'm sorry."

"It's okay. Don't be sorry. You didn't know." His voice is tight, as though he's on the edge of losing his shit.

"Yeah, but now I do. And if it were me in your shoes, I'd turn me down too."

I pick up my beer bottle from the coffee table. "Well, I need to go get some work done. Thank you for dinner, especially since it was my favorite."

The tension in his shoulders relaxes a little. "It was my pleasure."

"And thanks for letting me stay here, giving up your bed. I know this isn't easy for either of us. But I do want to thank you for putting me up."

His gaze meets mine, earnestness in those depths. "Eden, I would never let you stay somewhere that would be dangerous for you. I..." He stops and looks away for a moment. "Anyway, you're welcome. Let me know if you need anything. And don't forget to stay away from the windows."

"Thanks, I will." I turn and slowly make my way down the hall, weighed down by disappointment, guilt, and the whole situation.

Not only am I still without a speaker, but all of those feelings that I swore to everyone—including me—I'd never feel for Chase Hanover ever again have come roaring back with a vengeance.

All I want to do is wrap him in my arms and never let anyone hurt him again.

Tonight, the real Chase emerged from the shadows momentarily.

Kind, generous, and funny. Never mind that he only gets hotter with age.

The one that remembers my favorite meal.

The one I fell in love with all those years ago.

For his own wife and teammate to treat him the way they did makes me want to throat punch them. Well, the teammate anyway, since he's still among the living.

It's not quite seven o'clock and at home, when work calls my name, I always come running.

But for the first time in a long time, I ignore the call. I change into some lounge clothes and climb into bed.

Staring at the ceiling, I listen to the thunder, howling wind, and rain as it thrashes against the house. I can only imagine what a mess the storm will leave behind.

Sleep eludes me so I read, but even the spicy, football romance can't keep my mind from wandering back to Chase and the way he looked telling me his story.

It makes my heart ache to know that Chase has been portrayed as the villain, when he'd actually been the victim.

But it's easy to do since dead women don't speak.

And even if they did, it's doubtful Heather would have stood up for Chase. Especially if it would give her negative attention.

Dear Lord, please don't strike me down for thinking ill of the dead.

Then there's Ty Richardson. Unfortunately, it doesn't surprise me that he's involved in all of this.

Because if anyone should feel guilty about how the situation played out, it's that asshole. But knowing how he is, I'm positive he doesn't feel one ounce of regret or remorse.

Maybe he'd be a better baseball player if he wasn't so busy screwing other guys' wives.

I toss and turn for a bit longer, until finally around one o'clock, I'm sick of lying in bed.

Anxiety makes the walls close in, and the need to get out of this room is a priority.

Opening the door, I listen for Chase.

Other than the storm noise, it's quiet. I tiptoe out and shut the door quietly behind me.

The tile beneath my feet is freezing as I move quickly toward the open living space where Chase is lying on the couch.

A couch way too small for a man his size. His feet hang off one end, and one arm hangs down toward the floor.

But his soft snores keep me moving quietly as I continue a tour of the house.

I cross through the kitchen and head down a darkened hallway. There's an elevator, a room that looks like an office, and a single door at the end of the hall.

Curious, I turn the knob, and the door opens to an enclosed staircase leading down into darkness.

Fear skitters down my spine, and every bad horror movie I've ever watched runs through my head.

Chuckling, I roll my eyes at my melodramatics and flip on the lights. When I get to the bottom of the staircase, my jaw drops.

Holy shit.

There's a whole other house down here. Living room,

kitchen, small eating area off the kitchen, and other rooms down a hallway.

I peek in the first room and turn on the lights. The huge space is full of state-of-the-art gym equipment.

So, this is how Chase stays in such great shape.

Every piece of exercise equipment needed for arms, legs, and any other muscle group is arranged circuit style.

Along the mirrored wall are racks of weighted plates and dumbbells. In the back corner is an open area with mats that are perfect for yoga.

"Ah, yes. Maybe some yoga will help me sleep."

I choose a mat and sit cross-legged on it, closing my eyes, focusing on my breathing.

The tension in my body begins to dissipate with each breath.

In this space, away from Chase, away from being able to hear the storm outside, I can finally relax.

Usually, I follow a yoga sequence I know in my head, making sure I do each and every one properly.

But right now? That sounds exhausting, so I just let my body decide what feels good.

Thoughts of the charity event and what'll happen if I royally fuck it up try to invade my peace, but I push on them until they quiet down to a dull roar.

Keeping my eyes closed, I lift my arms and stretch side to side.

I move into child's pose, relishing the stretch and letting the feel of it sink into my muscles.

Lifting up, I move into another pose, holding the stretch for several seconds.

In the mirror, a motion catches my eye.

I gasp when I see Chase leaning against the doorjamb

watching me. His arms are crossed over his bare chest, and he has a pair of gray sweatpants on.

Son of a bitch. Those pants really are like lingerie for men.

They don't hide a damn thing.

I clear my throat. "Hey, did I wake you?"

He shakes his head, his gaze raking down my body from the top of my head to the tip of my toes.

It feels like he has branded me by the way my skin burns under his heated stare.

"Nah. I woke up thirsty and couldn't get back to sleep, so I thought I'd come down and lift some weights," he says, but doesn't move farther into the room.

I stand and smooth a hand down my shirt. "Yeah, I couldn't sleep either. Sometimes yoga helps relax me enough to fall asleep. But I can go so I'm not in your way."

He pushes off the door and starts toward me.

His walk is almost predatory and makes my heart pound in my ears.

I bite my lip, my feet glued to the floor, caught up in the laser-beam trap of his stare.

He stops in front of me, so close I have to tilt my head back. I look up to find his strong jaw tight and his eyes dark with desire.

"You've been in my way since you set foot on the island, Eden. Plaguing me at every turn. You've got me all confused. You torment me."

With every sentence, he moves closer, until his lips are so close to mine, I can smell the mint of his toothpaste and the soap on his skin.

I clench my thighs to relieve the pressure building between my legs. His words mesmerize me.

"I want nothing more than to take you upstairs and fuck you until we can't remember our names. But—"

My stomach jumps in anticipation at his words, making me inhale sharply.

I lay my fingertips on his lips.

"No buts. I want that too, Chase."

The huskiness in my voice and the fire between my legs is familiar. Chase is the only man that makes me feel like I'm going to spontaneously combust.

One hand cups my cheek before he slides it into my hair. He fists the strands and pulls gently, making our gazes meet head-on.

"Are you sure you want this? If I kiss you, I won't stop."

"Okay."

"I won't stop until I've tasted your pussy and filled you with my cum."

His words alone make me want to explode.

I run my hands over his chest then over his shoulders and hold on, his scar a small bump under my palm.

"Yes, I want this. I want you, Chase. But it's just sex. It can't be anything more than just sex. You're never coming back to New York, and I'll never set foot on this island again."

"Just sex. For the last time. Works for me."

The words barely pass his lips before he crushes his mouth to mine in a soul-searing kiss.

His lips are soft, full, and coaxing. He consumes me, drinks me in, pulls me under until I can barely stand on my own.

He bands an arm around my waist and pulls me up against him, his cock hard and insistent against my belly.

I need to feel him inside me, the weight of his body on me.

As much as my toys are good to get me off, there's no substitute for a hot, hard man.

Especially when the man is Chase Hanover.

Without breaking the kiss, he moves us over to one of the weight benches where one section of it is lifted into an inclined position. "Sit down," he murmurs against my lips. "And lean back."

His commands are hot as hell, and I follow his instructions eagerly.

Our eyes lock as he kneels in front of me, spreading my legs apart.

His wide palms run up my thighs and under the legs of my shorts until his fingers reach the edge of my panties.

With his fingertips, he rubs along the edge, teasing me next to where I want those fingers the most.

Back and forth, his finger runs along the elastic edge before hooking the waistband of my shorts and pulling them down my legs.

I'm bare and wide open to him, and he stares down at me, his gaze so intense that shyness reaches out and tries to take hold of me.

But the hungry look in his eyes gives me the confidence to keep my legs open so he can see my most intimate place.

He licks his lips and smiles up at me. "Hmmm...your pussy is even better than I remembered. Eden, how is it fair that you've only gotten more beautiful over the years?"

I gulp air, trying like hell to keep breathing so I don't pass out and fall onto the floor.

Chase has done little more than caress my thighs and take off my shorts and yet I'm breathing as though I've run a marathon.

All twenty-six miles of it in record time.

My hands grip the edge of the bench, and I fight the urge to squirm.

He runs a fingertip through my wetness, brushing my clit with his knuckle.

My hips jerk up when he makes a second pass over that super sensitive bundle of nerves.

"Yeah, that feels good, doesn't it? I can tell by how wet you are."

"Yes," I say breathlessly.

He pushes one finger into me slowly a couple of times before adding another one and crooking them, hitting that all important spot deep inside me.

"Oh God."

I bite my lip hard and buck my hips up, wanting more.

And he knows it.

"You want more, don't you?" he asks with a dark chuckle, adding another finger, his gravelly whisper raking over my skin.

"Yessss."

Of their own volition, my hips rock up to meet his hand as he finger fucks me.

I lean my head back, relishing the feeling of being full.

But I still want more.

I want his cock to stretch and fill me.

I want more than anything to have that connection with him again.

Chase leans forward, his tongue flicking my clit. Once. Twice, followed by a long, slow lick.

He continues this torturous rhythm for several moments until I'm teetering on the edge.

It doesn't take much more of his magical tongue before my orgasm bears down on me like an out-of-control freight train.

The overwhelming sensation of his mouth sucking me and his fingers filling me is too much for me to handle.

I bury my hands in his hair, my nails raking his scalp as I can do nothing more than release incoherent moans into the quiet of the room.

My whole world is centered between my legs, and everything else falls away.

I ride out wave after wave of pleasure.

When I finally stop seeing stars, Chase sits back on his haunches, licking his lips.

"You taste even sweeter than before."

"I don't think I've ever come so hard before."

The grin on his face is downright dirty, making my core clench.

"Oh baby, that was just the appetizer."

SIXTEEN
chase

MY PLAN HAD BEEN to stay away from Eden for the rest of the time we're trapped together.

No more meals together, no more talks, no more "checking to see how you're doing," which is code for my lame attempts to see her.

After our near miss last night, I planned out the whole thing.

But having a plan hasn't made my anxiety dissipate, so I do what I always do when I need to get out my frustration and sex isn't on the menu.

I head to my gym to work out.

My plan goes straight to hell when I find Eden doing yoga poses in my gym.

Son of a bitch.

How is a horny-ass man supposed to turn away from all the bending and stretching while she's in tiny shorts and a T-shirt?

And why do I find her bare feet the sexy cherry on top?

She's always been in great shape, but still has all those womanly curves about her.

Curves that have filled out more over the years, and watching her, I have to admit Eden Mitchell has the best body I've ever seen, hands down.

And I've had swimsuit models.

They don't hold a candle to the woman doing a downward dog in my home gym.

I've reached the point of no return.

When I advance on her and she doesn't back away, when her eyes light up with lust, I know there's no going back.

And once she gives me that consent? All bets are off. I don't care what rules she made.

I should walk away.

But with the taste of her on my tongue and her hand in mine, there's no way I'm walking away now.

I want her in my bed right now and not for sleeping.

At least not until she's had several orgasms.

But Eden being Eden, she has plans of her own, if the sparkle in her eye is any indication.

When she drops to her knees, I toss out my playbook for good. She tugs on the legs of my pants, freeing my commando erection.

"What are you doing?" I ask roughly.

"Getting *my* appetizer."

She glances down and her eyes widen on my shaft. "Holy shit. When did you do this?"

Her thumb rubs over the ball of the barbell piercing behind the head of my dick.

"Six months ago. I lost a bet."

She grins. "Well, lucky me. I've heard things about piercings."

I raise a brow. "Have you now?"

"How does it feel?"

"During sex?"

"Yeah."

I run my thumb over her bottom lip. "I don't know. We'll find out together."

Her mouth drops open. "You haven't had sex in six months?"

"Nope."

She tilts her head. "You're not lying to me?"

My chuckle comes out strained. "I wouldn't lie about sex."

"Well, then,"—her eyes light up with desire and glee—"I can't tell you how happy I am to hear that."

She grips my shaft and tugs down to the root. "Now, enough talking."

With a lick of her lips, she looks up at me from under those long lashes when her lips close over the tip. She goes down and back up in one smooth motion.

"Hmmm...I've missed this. But it's even better with this new addition."

She holds my gaze and swirls her tongue around the metal ball, licking the precum from the seam.

I grab ahold of her hair, the blonde strands spilling in a messy fountain over my fist and down her back.

"Fuck. Just think how good that's going to feel when I slide it inside your pussy."

Her hot mouth closes around my cock, her moan like a vibration around it. The wet heat is like heaven.

Eden on her knees in front of me, her beautiful mouth wrapped around my shaft, is the most erotic picture. Even better than in my fantasies I've had of her when we were apart.

She moans, and the vibration at the back of her throat heightens the sensation of being in her mouth.

With her head bobbing up and down, tongue flat against the bottom of my cock, the suction hollowing out her cheeks, I'm racing to the edge faster than I want to go.

If this is our last time together, I want to brand her as mine.

I want to ruin her so she never forgets me.

Other feelings I don't want to acknowledge fill my chest, but I ignore them and let go.

Closing my eyes, I focus on the feeling of her lips wrapped around me and her mouth sucking me off.

But when the tingle starts at the base of my spine, I ease back from her hungry mouth.

"Eden, baby. Stand up."

She wipes at her mouth with the back of her hand and stands. Her eyes gleam with desire, and her lips are slick.

She looks hot as hell.

"But I'm enjoying myself."

I cup her face in my hands and meet her eyes. "Me too, but when I come, I want to be inside you. Feel you clench around my cock. But stay right here."

Moving quickly to the bathroom I installed in the gym, I rummage through a drawer and find the foil disk I'm looking for.

Eden stands where I left her, in all her naked glory.

Shapely legs, high breasts with dusky pink tips that make me want to set up camp there and just lap at them all day.

She's curvy in all the right places, and it makes me harder than I thought possible just looking at her.

Yep, hands down.

She has a body men would kill for, and she doesn't even know it.

"God, you're stunning."

She looks at me from under her lashes and smiles. It's a smile full of heat and dirty promises.

With that smile, I'm a goner.

Hook, line, and sinker.

"Thank you."

Her response is soft, almost shy, and at total odds with the lust in her eyes.

I walk over to the weight bench and sit down. Her gaze lands on my lap, hungry eyes on my cock.

She doesn't even have to touch me for it to twitch, wanting her attention.

"Come here, gorgeous."

With a grace and elegance one is only born with, she walks to me. Her eyes are still full of fire as she keeps them steady on me.

When she stops between my spread apart knees, I reach up and cup the back of her neck, pulling her down for a kiss.

My tongue slides against hers as she moves closer into me, her hands landing on my shoulders.

Her fingernails dig into my skin, a biting pain mixing with the pleasure of her nipples brushing against my chest.

Those sweet buds harden against my skin, and with my free hand, I roll one and pinch lightly.

She moans into my mouth, her nails digging deeper. "Chase, please fuck me," she groans against my lips.

I pull back and tuck a lock of hair behind her ear. "You need to come again, don't you?"

A little moan escapes her as she nods.

With my teeth, I rip open the foil package and suit up as quick as I can.

She moves her hips over mine, and I line my cock up against her pussy, fighting back the urge to slam her down on me.

Sinking down, she takes me into her body inch by mother-fucking inch.

She leans her head back and moans. "Oh God. That feels incredible. I can feel every inch of you."

"You like this hard cock buried in your tight cunt, don't you?"

Her answer is nothing more than a moan.

My hands grip her hips, watching where my dick disappears into her pussy.

The sight is so fucking hot, and the feeling of being inside Eden again after so many years makes me feel alive.

As though the four years since we last had sex have been black and white and now the world around us is in sparkling color.

Sex with Eden had been an experience like no other before. But now?

Now, I'm afraid I'm the one who's ruined.

I flex my fingers against her skin, the urge to slam up into her almost more than I can bear.

It's pure heaven and pure hell.

Glancing up, seeing her positioned above me—eyes closed, lips parted, looking like the fucking goddess she is—I wonder how the hell I ever let her go.

What man doesn't want to see this picture every day of his life?

When our hips meet, she leans forward, her forehead against mine. "Chase," she says breathlessly. "I've missed you. I missed us."

I know what she means.

It's always been more than sex between us, from the very first time.

I don't—can't—respond. I just lift her up and down, making us both moan.

She takes over, pushing up with her legs and lowering herself back down.

With each bounce, she moves a bit faster, her hands gripping my shoulders. I lean my head back, enjoying her taking the lead, my hands on the curve of her hips.

As she moves over me, my hands roam all over soft skin.

I want to touch everywhere I can while I have her.

She slams down on me and does a little hip swivel, taking me even deeper into her body.

My fucking eyes cross. "Fuck me, Eden. That feels amazing."

Spurred on by my praise, she adds that swivel when I least expect it.

Her pussy clenches around me, and her skin takes on the sexiest blush. Her breath comes faster, and her body tells me she's chasing down her next orgasm.

I want to help her catch it.

Leaning forward, I band my arms around her waist, bringing our chests flush together.

I drive into her from below, relentless in my pursuit to push us both over the edge and fall into the oblivion of bliss.

She leans her head back and moans, each thrust causing her tits to bounce against my chest.

"Yes, Chase, just like that. Don't stop."

"Not a chance in hell I'm stopping."

The bench squeaks beneath us with each pounding her body takes from me.

A few more thrusts and she clamps down on me, my name on her lips, echoing off the walls of the large room. I slam up into her one last time and let go.

I come so hard, all I see are stars.

She drops her head to my shoulder, both of us panting.

"Oh my God. That was...well, let's just say, the piercing was a good idea." Her words are muffled against my skin, and I chuckle.

"Not too bad."

Not too bad if mind-blowing isn't your thing.

Eden's head pops up, and she look down at me with a raised brow. "Excuse me?"

The haughty tone of her voice and slight lift of her chin are sexy and adorable all at once.

As usual where Eden is concerned, I'm royally fucked.

But I play it casual because that's all we'll ever be.

"I'm just saying you may need to show me how you've upped your sex game again. Not sure I caught it the first time."

I drop kisses along the tops of her tits. "Besides, I know we said just once, but maybe we could amend that to one night and you can show me your skills."

She purses those pillowy lips and narrows her eyes, before letting out an exaggerated sigh.

A sigh that makes said tits do amazing things.

"No, I can't possibly leave you wondering about my sex skills."

"We should probably get started on that."

She squirms in my lap, and my dick twitches inside her. "Seems like it. But I think we need to try another room. Different scenery and all."

"I like the way you think." I smack her ass, making her yelp, but when her pussy clenches around me, I know she didn't hate it.

She lifts off me, and I make quick work of getting rid of the condom. When I come out of the bathroom, she's getting dressed.

I lean against the door, arms crossed over my chest. "You know, it's going to be hard to prove to me how good you are with clothes on."

She looks down at her shirt and then back up at me, a wicked gleam in her eye. With a tilt of her head, she says, "I don't know. I remember there were a few times we had sex fully clothed."

Memories of being in the back seat of my car, in the bathroom at a couple of frat parties, and that one time in the movie theater have me on my way to being fully hard again. "True enough."

I push off the door and stalk toward her. "But given the fact that it's just us in the house, I don't think we're going to have to worry about getting caught."

"True enough."

She pulls the T-shirt back over her head and stands before me naked once again. "Better?" she asks, a hand on her hip, sassiness radiating off her.

My grin hurts my face. "Much."

She bites her lip, holding back a grin before she takes off toward the stairs.

I'm caught off guard, but I catch up with her quickly, wrapping an arm around her waist and hauling her up against me.

Her laughter makes my heart light, and I'll always remember the sound of it.

I pick her up in a fireman's hold, surprising a squeak out of her. All I can do is laugh at her halfhearted protests to be put down.

I can't remember the last time I felt this free.

SEVENTEEN

chase

A LONG, low rumble of thunder wakes me up.

The warmth of Eden wakes my lower half up as well.

I check the time on my phone to find it's nearly eight in the morning.

Outside, beyond the sliding glass doors of my bedroom, the storm continues to rage but with much less intensity than yesterday.

I stare at the ceiling and wonder if the mess of debris outside is as bad as the mess inside my head.

Eden and I spent the night seeing how sturdy my furniture is, pushing past limits and breaking down barriers between us.

When we finally made it to the bed, we talked until we couldn't keep our eyes open.

It was the best night of my life with anyone, and yet I lie here with a cloud of doubt trying to rain on my parade.

Eden's warmth surrounds me and makes me feel all sorts of things I decided I'd never feel for her again.

It has to be just sex.

It has to be.

She deserves better than a man who does nothing but hurt

the ones he loves. I'm a wrecking ball when it comes to emotions.

My own father had told me that enough times, hadn't he?

After my mother died from complications of the flu, the doctors said it was a rare situation with her lungs, and the pneumonia was just too much for her.

That didn't deter my father from telling me it was my fault since she'd gotten the virus from me.

And the man had a field day when the media dug up the past and paid him a visit.

No problem taking money from the vultures to go on record and call his son a selfish bastard who only thought of himself. And two women were dead because of it.

Until the day he died a couple of years ago, my father called me a killer.

Never mind that I'd lost my mom and my wife.

After my mom died, I worked my ass off with my grades and playing baseball to get a scholarship to anywhere that would take me away from the hell my home life had become.

But in college, I let loose. Partied a little too hard on a couple of occasions.

Then my coach sat me down and chewed my ass out. Made me realize I was about to lose my scholarship and my place on the team.

That would mean going back home.

And that wasn't happening.

That same day, I'd met Eden.

As soon as I met her, I knew she'd change my life.

And she did, for better or worse.

I still celebrated victories with the guys, but they were much tamer versions because I always brought my girl with me. We'd been inseparable.

Until I'd done what I always do and fucked it up.

She needed me when her mother had fallen ill after we'd graduated.

I tried to convince her to come with me, but she said regardless of how shitty her mom could be, she was still her mom.

And what had I done?

I wish I could say I'd understood, but the pain of losing my own mom was still too fresh I guess.

Nope, that's not what I did.

I'd thought of only myself first, just like my father always said I did, and went to Los Angeles without her.

But the truth is, all I've ever wanted is to be wherever Eden was.

I'd close my eyes and imagine I was somewhere with her.

The beach, her tiny off-campus apartment, baseball games, driving around singing to the radio.

And yet I'd walked away. It hadn't mattered that she'd agreed and said I should go. She'd wanted me to have that shot.

It was selfless of her. Just like what she's trying to do now with her business.

And here I am—the bastard still too selfish to help her.

All because I'd married a woman I never should have—but it would be great PR for me, so I did.

And not only had someone gotten hurt, but someone died.

Just like my mother.

I run a finger down the soft skin of her arm, pain heavy in my chest.

There's no way I can start anything with Eden again. Ever.

She makes me feel things I don't deserve.

To get involved with her again would be a disaster.

Just like everything else good in my life.

Dramatic much, Hanover?

I sigh and run a hand down my face.

Eden stirs, her fingers trailing across my stomach, nails lightly scratching across my skin. "Good morning, handsome."

Her voice is husky with sleep, and with her hand inching its way down south, I push away thoughts of anything other than right now.

With the way our past has played out, I can't think about our future.

"Morning, Sunshine."

Her nickname rolls off my tongue, and it feels right, especially when I feel her smile against my chest.

I look down at the top of her head, fascinated by the different colors of blonde swirled through her hair. "How did you sleep?"

She perches her chin on my chest. "Better than I have in a long time. You?"

"Like a baby."

And it's true.

I'm hit with the realization it both comforts me and scares the shit out of me to know I actually slept so soundly.

It feels a lot like she's the reason why.

Her smile is shy. "Good, I'm glad to hear it."

The smile falters just a bit, and she runs a fingertip along my chest. "What's on your mind?"

The mix of green and blue in her eyes holds me captive.

God, she's the most beautiful woman I've ever known.

Inside and out.

On the outside, she's all traffic-stopping beauty.

On the inside, the woman is smart, compassionate, and giving.

She's always been that way, and it doesn't surprise me that she's had success in event management, bad judgment calls notwithstanding.

I personally know the guys that hired her to do their event don't hire just anybody to do something that's important to them.

They expect only the best.

Her rare combo of beauty and brains is enough to knock me to my knees.

I want to be her hero, be the man that I wasn't years ago.

But the hollow, sick feeling in my stomach roars back anytime I think of going back to NYC and the paparazzi following me again.

The constant dodging them, flashbulbs in my face, camping out in front of my building, and asking questions that were crude at best and downright hateful at worst.

They made my life hell for far too long. But fear weighs me down and keeps me broken.

It's best to remember what this is all about with Eden.

Because I can't go back to that hell. I can't be that hero for her.

We can just have some fun while we're stuck together.

Just sex.

It is just sex.

My hand slides down and cups her ass under the sheet. "You're the only thing on my mind." I squeeze, and she lets out a tiny squeak before it turns into a soft moan when my fingers drift down and close to where she's already wet.

"I like the way you think."

With that spark in her eye, she holds my gaze, dropping kisses across my chest.

Her long hair trails over my nipples as she drops kisses on my scar.

I close my eyes and swallow hard against the range of emotions that whip through me and end up lodging in my throat.

The few women I've been with since my surgery have made sure to steer clear of my shoulder scar, as though if they don't acknowledge it, the pink slash of puckered skin isn't there and I can be their flawless, hot athlete conquest.

The fact that Eden gives it more attention than the smooth skin around it soothes away those edges that make me forget I'm lucky to be alive.

She makes her way to one of my nipples, where she swirls her tongue around it. It hardens, and the feeling of it makes me grunt.

I squeeze her ass and pull her closer to me. With one leg already slung up over mine, it's easy for her to grind her wet heat against my thigh.

"Hmmm..." she murmurs as she moves to the other nipple and laps at it like her life depends on it.

Damn, she knows how to use that tongue to make me come unglued.

Unable to just lie there any longer, I flip her onto her back and settle between her legs.

Her lips curve into a smile that lights up her face in the shadowy room. "I like this position even better."

I kiss her hard once. "Want to do something with me?"

She chuckles. "If you don't know by now I'm saying yes, then I'm not very good at this."

"You're amazing at this. *We're* amazing at this. But that's not what I mean." I pause, knowing I need to ask but not sure if I want to even hear the answer. "Do you trust me?"

She bites her lip and searches my eyes for a moment before nodding slowly, silently.

"Okay, stay right here. Close your eyes."

There are a thousand questions in her eyes, but they slide closed after a second.

I climb off the bed and walk into my closet, on the hunt for what I want.

I come back out of the closet, then hurry out to the kitchen.

When I walk back into the bedroom, I find that Eden hasn't moved, her eyes still closed, hands crossed casually over her belly.

With the even motion of her chest, I wonder if she's fallen asleep on me.

Until she smiles.

"Going to just stand there and stare at me?"

The teasing lilt of her voice propels me into gear again. "Oh, I'm going to do a lot more than stare at you, babe."

"Am I going to need a safe word?"

I chuckle. "I don't think so. But just in case, say 'red leather.'"

She cracks open a lid. "Red leather?"

"Yep. Do you still trust me?"

"Yes."

"Then close your eyes."

She closes her eye again, a small smile on her lips. "Hmmm...I'm intrigued."

"Keep your eyes closed, Eden."

"They are, Chase."

I smile and shake my head.

Such a smart mouth.

I toss a couple of my silk ties on the floor and sit with a bowl of ice at the end of the bed.

"What is that?" she asks, lifting her head slightly off the pillow.

"You'll find out soon enough."

"You're going to make me wait?"

"Patience, my love. Patience."

She mumbles something under her breath and lays her head back down.

Taking one of the ties, I move to her head. "Lift up."

She lifts her head and I tie the fabric into a knot behind her head. "Is that too tight?"

Biting her lip, she shakes her head.

With another tie in hand, I kneel on the bed and run the back of my hand down the outside of her arm, caressing it along the way.

Goose bumps break out over her skin, making her gasp.

The breathy sound hits me right in the gut.

Just to hear it again, I repeat the motion on her other arm before lifting them both over her head and securing her wrists around the wooden post of the headboard.

I pull gently on the silk. "Is this okay?"

She nods, her breathing picking up slightly.

I've done little more than caress her soft, smooth skin and yet the air is so thick with sexual anticipation, I can barely breathe.

I move down to the end of the bed and pick up another tie.

With the narrow end of it, I use the silk to tease the inside of one thigh. A small moan escapes her, and her legs widen a bit.

I draw figure eights down her legs until I reach her ankle, which I tie to the post.

By the time I give her other leg the same teasing treatment and tie the other ankle, Eden's breaths are on the verge of pants.

"Last chance, baby. Do I stop or do I continue?"

"Don't you dare stop now, Chase Hanover. I'll kill you."

"That's my girl."

I back off the bed and grab a condom from the nightstand.

"Chase, lift the blindfold, please."

I frown. What had changed her mind?

When I push the tie up her forehead, our eyes meet. "You okay?"

She nods and licks her lips. "I'm on the pill. And I haven't been with anyone since my last physical." A sexy smile curves her lips. "Until now, that is."

We haven't been together with nothing between us since...

But I've never forgotten how amazing she felt around me and how I once thought I could die inside her and be perfectly happy with it.

I have to swallow before I can speak. "I had my physical last month and all tests were negative."

She nods once with a smile that's seductive and full of sin. Dropping her head back to the pillow, she declares. "I'm ready now."

I toss the condom aside and lower the tie back over her eyes.

Moving to the end of the bed, I take a moment and look down at her.

I have the best vantage point.

Eden's beautiful, without doubt, but a completely naked, vulnerable Eden?

It nearly kills me.

All the flushed, smooth skin, her curves, the high, full breasts that rise and fall with her breaths.

By the looks of her skin, she's turned on—that beautiful pale pink shade that makes something inside me swell.

I'm no longer a betting man, but I'd bet my left nut that none of the other men she's been with had noticed that simple but sexy little detail about her.

Mine.

But she isn't mine, and someday, some guy is going to make sure he keeps her for his own.

I can't be that guy. But until she leaves?

She's mine, all mine.

I want to devour her. I'm going to give her everything she can handle and then some.

Sliding a piece of ice from the bowl, I touch her skin just above her ankle with it.

"Oh, shit! That's cold." Eden tries to jerk away, but the motion only serves to tighten the tie and hold her in place.

"Be still, Sunshine."

Her breathing speeds up as I drag the ice up each leg, leaving a wet line on her skin.

I lie on my belly between her legs, and when I come to her apex—my heaven—I put the ice in my mouth and lean forward.

When my cold tongue touches her clit, she practically shoots off the bed.

"Chase!" She pants as my tongue flicks up and down her slit. The heat of her pussy clashing with the freezing ice heightens everything.

The ice melts quickly, the cold water dribbling down my chin as I continue to lick her.

She's so wet, I can't be sure where the water ends and her sweet desire begins.

The little nub of nerves hardens under my ministrations, a sure sign that she's close to coming.

She arches her back and moans when I insert a finger into her. When I curve my finger and move it slowly deep inside her folds, she tugs hard on the ties that bind her to the bed.

Eden murmurs incoherently, and I look up at her.

Her flushed skin, her curves all on display, her mouth in a perfect O.

I've never seen anything more exquisite.

"Let go, babe. Come in my mouth."

"Oh God..."

I dip another finger into her wetness and keep up the steady rhythm, moving in and out of her body, alternating between sucking and flicking her clit.

I want to drive her crazy, push her to that high peak and let her fly.

Her fingers wrap around the ties, her knuckles turning white when she cries out my name.

"Chase, oh God! I'm going to come...I..."

She trails off into a long, high-pitched moan. The walls of her wet heat clench down on my fingers, and her clit hums under my tongue as the orgasm takes over.

I stay where I am, only slowing down my motions when she shudders and her body stops vibrating.

Standing, I stroke my rock-hard dick, watching her catch her breath and relish in her post-orgasmic glow.

"Chase?"

"Yeah?"

"Need you," she pants out.

An overwhelming desire to take everything she'll give me brings out an animalistic need to mate with her.

She can't move her legs, but lifts her hips, as though offering herself to me.

My heart pounds at the sight, and if my girl needs me, I'm here to provide.

Truth be told, I need her too.

I need that connection with her. To know this isn't some surreal fantasy and I'll wake up soon.

And if it is? Don't bother ever waking me up.

Moving between her legs, I stroke the tip against her wet slit, teasing us both.

She squirms and moans underneath me. "Chase, please..."

I line up, and with one hard thrust, I'm fully seated inside her.

The need to pull out and slam back into her is overwhelming, but I stay still because I want to feel her wrapped around me for just a minute longer.

Her cunt clenches around me and the feel and heat of it all is so intense, I can't think.

Biology takes over, and I brace my arms beside her head, then let loose.

The headboard slams into the wall, echoing the rhythm we find and mingling with our moans.

I reach back and untie her ankles so she can wrap her legs around my waist.

That change in angle has me even deeper in her heat, unraveling quickly.

I grab the headboard for better leverage, and my hips slam into her.

"Yes, Chase. Fuck me harder," Eden cries out.

Her wish is my command.

Our bodies slap together, and her tits bounce in an erotic symphony.

I shove the blindfold up her forehead so I can see her eyes. I need to see them—see that connection we have.

When I look into her blue-green depths, I see desire, hope, love, her soul.

All the things I've been missing since we've been apart.

My name is a chant on her lips that lets me know all she can see or feel is me.

When her nipples harden and her pussy starts to clamp down around me, the tingling in my spine becomes more like a buzz.

Her thighs clench around my waist as though she's trying to squeeze the life out of me.

I'd die a happy man.

She thrashes her head and chants my name as I explode, spilling everything I have into her.

I see motherfucking comets, and I'm pretty sure the earth just moved off its axis.

We're both gasping for air when I lay my forehead on hers.

After a moment, I untie her wrists. They're slightly pink from where the fabric bit into her skin.

I bring one to my mouth and kiss it. "Do they hurt?" I ask, rubbing with my thumb.

"No, they're fine," she whispers, looping her arms around my neck.

She pulls me down, and her lips meet mine in a soft kiss. "That was...I don't have any words that describe that."

"Earth-shattering? Mind-melting?"

She grins. "All of the above and then some."

Her grin becomes a shy smile, and with her finger, she traces my bottom lip before bringing her gaze up to mine. "I've missed you."

My heart swells, and for a moment I don't know if I can speak without saying all the things I want to say.

Like... *I've never stopped loving you.*

It was a mistake to ever let you go years ago.

I'm a broken man and I don't deserve you, but love me anyway.

But our little informal agreement doesn't include anything but sex.

And I *am* damaged goods.

I never should have looked in her eyes when I came inside her. But since I did, I have to remember I'm not fit for more than a good fuck.

I should say something that will take that look out of her eyes.

The look she used to give me back in college, just before she said those three little words that meant everything to me.

That still mean everything to me.

But that I no longer deserve.

I should say something like, "Yeah, my dick missed you too."

Or something equally as douchey. Something the asshole the world sees me as would say.

Instead, the words that come out of my mouth are...

"I missed you too. More than you'll ever know."

EIGHTEEN

eden

"SO, WHAT ARE WE WATCHING?"

"I don't know. Have anything in mind?"

Chase looks over at me and bobs his brows lecherously. "I've always got you in my bed on the brain."

I shove at him with a laugh. "Oh my God, you're as bad as you were in college."

"No way. I'm worse now, making up for lost time with you."

Chase grips my wrist as I try to pull it away and drops a kiss on the inside of it.

I bite back a gasp, but the rush of heat that lands between my legs can't be stopped.

"Where you're concerned, Eden? You're always on my mind."

He says it casually, but the intense look he gives me rocks my world, and my heart slams against my ribs.

"You really mean that?"

"Yeah, I really do."

We stare at each other until I feel the sting of tears behind my eyes. I roll my lips inward to try and hold them back.

When I know I'm not going to cry, I say, "I tried not to think of you, but I always did."

He brushes a lock of hair away from my face, a smile spreading on his lips. "You know what we should watch?"

I exhale quietly, half of me relieved he's changing the subject, the other half of me wishing we would talk about things.

"What's that?"

"*The Shawshank Redemption.* It brings back some unforgettable memories."

"Yeah, it does." I smile and pull a blanket off the back of the sofa, drawing it around me.

My heart beats a little faster looking at him in nothing but a pair of jeans. That sculpted chest and tousled hair drive me wild.

"Lots of studying everything but the books."

"Do you remember where we were when we watched *Shawshank* together the first time?" I ask.

He smiles. "Hell, yeah, I do. In my dorm room. My roommates were gone that night, and we had the whole place to ourselves."

My smile matches his. "It was our first time."

He chuckles, and his eyes take on a hazy quality as though he's plucking the memories from his brain. "There were a lot of firsts that night. First time I'd had sex in my dorm room."

I sit up straighter. "What? Now I know you're lying."

He shakes his head. "No, I'm serious. Before you, any girl I met, I went back to her place."

"Why?" I can't hide the bewilderment in my voice.

He shrugs. "It was easier to leave in the morning. Besides, for a guy, the walk of shame in the morning is more like the walk of fame, depending on the girl. And I didn't like the thought of kicking the girl out in the morning."

It dawns on me what he was saying. "Then why did... Oh."

"Yeah. Oh."

My throat grows thick. Holy shit. How did I miss that back then?

I look away and clear my throat. "So, uh. What were the other firsts?"

"Well, let's see. First in my dorm, first time I'd cooked breakfast for a girl." He looks back over at me. "First time I'd ever wanted to please the girl more than I wanted to please myself."

I bite my lip, my heartbeat quickening, unsure of what to say. "I didn't know all that."

He laughs. "Well, you weren't supposed to. We'd known each other all of what, a week? We'd had two dates."

"That wasn't even a date that night."

"No, we were studying lit, right?"

"It is why we were watching *Shawshank* after all."

"Well, we didn't watch much, did we? I had to watch the movie again later to know what was going on."

"If it makes you feel better, so did I."

We laugh, but when our eyes meet, the air thickens with that electric tension always between us.

It's an intimate feeling that makes me feel safe and desired.

Lifting a hand, he cups the side of my face, his palm warm against my cheek. I close my eyes and lean into it, my own emotions rioting through my body.

Desire, hope, regret, and that one feeling I refuse to name when it comes to this man

No matter how much I want it.

My heart says, *go for it.*

My head says, *girl, you better run.*

And all the things he says to me don't help the chaos in my head.

I'm totally screwed.

"Eden, I—"

The doorbell rings, and Chase narrows his eyes. "Who the hell would be out now?"

"Maybe the sheriff? I can't imagine who else would be out in this."

He goes to the front door, and through the back windows, I watch the dissipating storm with a sense of dread.

Unable to sit still, I follow the voices to the front door and stop when I come around the corner.

Nate, Charley, and a man I recognize as another baseball player, Lucas Raines, are standing in the foyer, dripping wet.

Everyone stops talking when they see me.

They look back and forth between me and Chase, who stands at the front door in only jeans.

Jeans I just now realize have the top button undone.

Chase's gaze darts down my body. His eyes meet mine again, brows high.

Cover up, he mouths to me.

I look down.

Oh, shit.

My nipples decide to make an appearance under the thin T-shirt, and it's not even cold.

"Whoops." I tighten the blanket around me to stop giving the neighbors a show.

"Going to introduce me, Hanover?" Lucas asks.

Chase narrows his eyes at him. "If you stop leering, asshole."

Lucas just laughs and steps forward, hand outstretched. "Hey there, Lucas Raines."

I shake his hand, keeping the blanket tight around me. "Legendary Bull Sharks pitcher, I know. It's a pleasure to meet you. I'm Eden Mitchell."

Chase sighs. "Come on in and tell me why you're bothering me."

Given my job, I go into hostess mode.

Though I usually do it fully clothed, in my business suits that are my armor.

Without those clothes, I'm nothing more than a clumsy girl not sure of what to do next.

"How about I get you some towels and make some coffee?"

I rush down the hallway to Chase's room to put on some actual clothes and grab some towels.

A few moments later, our visitors are drying off and coffee is brewing.

With some time alone in the kitchen, I check my phone to see what I've missed.

It's a wonder it isn't in pieces after seeing all the texts and emails that have blown it up.

As the scent of coffee fills the air, I scroll through my phone looking for the most important messages first.

I have a million messages from Katie about things at the office and her headway on finding a speaker for the event.

Her texts start out a bit panicky and grow more worried until she finally threatens to come down here and find me to make sure I am not dead.

Then they become resigned to the fact that she can't get here anyway and I'm either dead, have no cell service, or am tied up with Chase.

She has no clue how she nailed her last comment.

I laugh and decide to put her out of her misery.

> Eden: Hey, Katie. I'm alive and fine. The storm is dying down here but the bridge is still closed.

Katie: Oh thank God! So you're alive and have cell service. Which means one thing.

Eden: Stop

Katie: You were tied up with Chase, weren't you? And I don't mean you were having a conversation.

Eden: When you say tied up, what do you mean?

Katie: Girl. Details. Pronto.

Katie: *Gif of woman with grabby hands*

Eden: She looks like you. Pink coat and all!

I laugh, but I'm not ready to give Katie details just yet.

Eden: Okay, let's get back on track here.

Katie: Party pooper.

She texts me some updates on a few of the other contracts we have going, and I give her direction on how to proceed on a few things.

Katie: One last thing. Did you check your email in between sex sessions? Probably not, but anyway, Marketing sent something to you.

I roll my eyes but can't stop the grin. I also have to keep this conversation on track.

Eden: I'm checking now.

I switch over to my email, and when I see the number of messages in my inbox, my shoulders slump.

It'll take me two days to get through all of these.

Scrolling, I look for an email from the head of marketing. When I find it and read it, I rub my forehead hard, trying to ward off the impending headache.

Hi Eden,

The deadline to get the brochures and other marketing materials out for the Pediatric Ball is quickly approaching. The drop dead date is in three days, unless we pay extra to do the express run with the printer. Can you send me the lineup of speakers ASAP? I'd like to save the department some money.

I look up from the phone when Charley walks into the kitchen and leans against the counter by the coffee station.

Shutting down the screen, I lay the phone on the bar. I can't deal with any of that right now.

I paste on my best hostess smile. "So, what brings you guys over here in the storm?"

She rolls her eyes. "Stewie got his car stuck in the sand. Nate wants to see if Chase can help."

"Stewie?"

"Local reporter. Always getting himself in jams."

"Well, that sounds like a problem."

She gestures to my head. "Headache?"

"Sort of. Headache-inducing email."

Charley nods and takes two cups from the mug tree. "Yeah, I recognize the look." She pours and slides one over to me. "I see it in the mirror every morning."

"Marketing is looking for an answer on some brochures for my big event so we can get them printed in time." I sigh.

"And I keep hoping Chase will decide he can be my speaker."

A tendril of steam rises and dissipates into the air as she sips her coffee. "Dragging his feet?"

"I don't know if it's that. He's got his reasons for not wanting to go back."

A hollow feeling hits my stomach thinking about Chase's story and yet what it means for me if he continues to say no.

"Hmmm...maybe Chase just needs the right incentive to go back to New York and help you."

"Be that as it may, I've got a business to save. And I need his help, but after what he's been through, I can't push him to say yes when he's not ready."

God, this is so complicated.

But what isn't complicated is the fact that I still have an event to manage, and I'm on the verge of losing not only the project, but my reputation and business.

"So, y'all were a thing once, right?"

I nod. "We dated in college. And then he was drafted to the majors and we broke up."

"So you haven't seen him in ten years?"

"No, the last time I saw him was four years ago. After his wife's funeral."

She makes a noncommittal noise as she sips her coffee.

"What?" I ask.

"I was just thinking how much fun we can have once you move here."

My eyes widen. "Move here? I'm not moving here."

She rolls her eyes and sets down her cup. "In the two times I've seen you two together, I've seen the way he looks at you."

Folding her arms over her chest, she smiles smugly. "Fifty bucks says you two realize how much you still love each other and you're living here inside a year."

I make the error of sipping my coffee just as she speaks.

I slap a hand over my mouth to keep from spitting coffee into her beautiful, but obviously crazy, face.

"I'm sorry," I say, wiping at my lip. "I'm not in love with Chase."

When she raises a brow, I bob my head side to side. "Okay, yes. Once upon a time in a land far, far away"— though not that far now that I think about it—"I was in love with Chase. Desperately. But that was years ago, and we were just kids in college."

She narrows her eyes. "Unless I miss my guess, you've rekindled those feelings since you've been here."

"How could you tell? I'm sure it wasn't my outfit that gave it away." My face heats. "Sorry about the eyeful."

Charley laughs and waves her hand. "Don't worry about it. I'm sure the guys enjoyed it."

"I wish I had your confidence when it comes to men."

"Nate's married but he isn't dead or blind. And Lucas is Lucas. Biggest playboy in the league."

I sigh. "I know, but still..."

"Here's the thing. It isn't confidence with men. It's being secure in the knowledge that Nate loves me. He shows me every day. Never lets me forget it. Because of that, I don't worry when he gets an eyeful of a beautiful woman's body. Especially one that doesn't notice any other man in the room." She nudges my arm. "And my husband wasn't the only one looking."

I set my cup down on the counter and drop my forehead to my hand. "I can't think, and this is what happens to me when I get around Chase and I don't know what he's thinking."

"So you're saying you become a twit when he's around and forget all about who you really are?"

I sigh and cover my face. "Something like that."

She pulls my hands away from my face. "Eden, you can handle this. You love that man in there and he loves you. I know because when he sees you, he can't take his eyes off you. And you're the same way."

"But, I can't get involved with him, Charley. I have a career to think of—a business. And it's in New York. A city Chase swears he'll never step foot back in after what happened with his late wife."

"Listen, I don't know the whole story on...well, any of it. You, him, the late wife. I know what I read in the papers, but I also know that what the papers write can be a lot of bullshit. So I don't put a lot of stock in that."

She leans on the counter. "But what I do put stock in is what I see. And I see two people who deserve another chance with each other."

"I don't know. I just don't think that's the case here. For either of us."

She glances up but lowers her voice. "Incoming. If you want to talk some more, I'll give you my number."

We're trading numbers when Nate and the man monopolizing my brain walk into the room—Chase now wearing a T-shirt—his gaze locking with mine.

"What are you two ladies chatting about in here?"

Charley smiles. "Just girl talk. What about you guys?"

"Well, I convinced Chase to help Stewie get his box car out of the sand," Nate says.

I look back and forth between them. "Box car?"

"Yeah, you know," Lucas says, "one of those little smart cars. Anyway, he got it stuck in the sand, and before the Atlantic comes and carries it away, I told him I'd see if Chase could use his truck to help him out."

Chase narrows his eyes at his friend. "Thanks for that, buddy."

"I'll go with you."

Wait, who said that? Had I said that?

All eyes turn to me.

Shit, I did say that out loud.

"No." Chase's tone brooks no argument.

I narrow my eyes at him. "What do you mean, no? Last I checked you weren't my keeper."

Chase crosses his arms over his chest, and we have a stare down.

"Um, we're going to get going," Charley says, pushing Nate and Lucas out of the room.

But she's petite and the two men built like brick houses barely budge.

"But Firefly, there's going to be fireworks here," Nate says.

Charley sighs. "We're going to have more than fireworks if you don't get your ass in gear. Come on."

The two men grumble but walk out as she waves. "We'll just let ourselves out."

Neither of us say a word, the front door closing the only sound in the house.

Chase breaks the silence first. "I'm not letting you go out in this. It's still dangerous."

I mimic his stance, crossing my arms over my chest.

"I'm not some simpering little woman, Chase. Haven't I proven that enough by now? And are you saying you're the only one that should go out in the dangerous weather? It's not safe for me, but magically safe for you?"

His jaw bunches, and a tic in his cheek tells me he's reining in his temper as best he can.

Join the club, buddy.

"No," he says, deceptive calm in his voice. "But I've been through a couple of these since I've been on the island. I think we've already established that you underestimate the weather."

My hands curl into fists, and I blow out a breath. "Yes, but I'll be with you. Just tell me where you need my help."

When he doesn't budge, I put a hand on my hip. "Fine, I'll just go sit in the truck and wait for you. Short of manhandling me, you can't make me get out."

I start toward the front door, when he catches my wrist and brings me up against his chest.

In his green eyes, it isn't so much anger I see as it is frustration and a healthy dose of fear.

"You drive me crazy, you know that?"

I give him a feline smile. "Same goes, Hanover."

He glances at my lips before meeting my eyes again. "Fine. But you have to do as I say, okay? It's easy to miscalculate the flooding here." He pauses. "Do you promise you'll listen?"

I hold up three fingers. "Scout's honor."

Before I can take my next breath, he has my face in his hands and kisses the hell out of me.

I slump against him, gathering a fistful of fabric with my hands.

Just when I think I'll pass out from lack of oxygen, he releases me.

"Let's go help this idiot and get back. We've got a few more rooms in this house to christen before the night's over."

NINETEEN

chase

THE WOMAN HAS ONLY BEEN BACK in my life for a couple of days, and she's already dug her way under my skin so deep that it makes me act a little crazy.

Between the incredible sex and her stubborn streak a mile wide, I don't know whether to fuck her or fight her.

Because she's right.

She can hold her own, and damned if she doesn't surprise me at every turn.

We're soaked to the bone in our clothes. Thankfully the worst of the storm moved out quickly, but the outer bands are still providing a shit ton of rain and wind.

Eden keeps Stewie calm and distracted while I hook the winch up to his box car as Nate calls it.

And he isn't wrong. It looks like a matchbox car but uglier.

Moments later, the matchbox car is out of harm's way from the angry waves that could have carried it away.

I send him on his way with a stern look and a growl that has him stammering he'll stay away from the beach until the storm is over.

The rain slows down considerably on our way back to the

house, but is still coming down sideways as wind gusts blow rain and sand across the road.

"Help me keep an eye out for debris."

"You got it."

I glance over at her as we drive down the road. She's looking out the side window, doing her best to see past the rain that pelts the glass.

Looking back in front of me, I give myself a mental shake to keep my shit together.

Contrary to the rules we set out, I want to spend more time with Eden.

And our time is coming to an end.

The storm is moving out and she'll be gone soon. I'm not ready to watch her leave again, even if I don't mind the view as she walks away.

But every time she leaves, she takes a piece of my heart with her.

A fact that I'm only just admitting to myself.

What's the worst that could happen if I were to do the speaking gig for her?

Yeah, there will be paparazzi, but if she's by my side, I can handle it.

I need to at least try.

"When did you say your speaking gig is in New York?"

Out of the corner of my eye, I see her head whip around to look at me. I glance over to find her mouth has dropped open slightly.

"Thirteen days, to be exact."

"Has your assistant gotten any new leads?"

Her shoulders slump, and she shakes her head. "No. And she's pretty resourceful, but no, nothing solid."

I tap my finger on the steering wheel as we ride down the nearly empty two-lane road.

Uneasiness still pushes in my chest, but the desire to be with Eden for a while longer is crowding that out.

"How much press will be there?"

Eden rolls her lips inward before answering. "Given the guest list and who the hosts are, I expect there to be a good bit of press. But they're restricted to the outside. There will be absolutely none inside."

"And you have security set up?"

"There will be a lot of high rollers there that night. Several big names from the business world, as well as a few celebrities. I've hired one of the top security firms around. Hudson was insistent on it."

"Yeah, he's a private guy."

She shifts slightly in her seat to face me. "Chase, I promise you, if you do this, I'll do whatever you need to feel comfortable being there. I promise I'll take care of you."

Pausing, she looks down before raising her eyes back to me. "But if the answer is still no, I truly understand."

I glance over at her and hold her gaze for a moment before looking back to the road. "I know you do. I appreciate it. If I consider it, when do you need my final answer?"

She sits up a little straighter, opening her mouth like she's going to say something, then shakes her head.

"Well, the sooner the better because I have some marketing materials I need to finalize. But I have a backup plan for that. The biggest thing is I need to let the guys know first."

I stop at a four-way stop and look over at her. "Give me 'til tomorrow?"

A small smile plays on her lips as she shifts back in her seat. "Absolutely."

We both know I'm halfway gone to saying yes.

But I need time to prepare myself for the inevitable questions I'll get, but that isn't the worst part.

It's the ramifications after the event that I worry about the most.

Will they dig up the old article with my father and call me a killer again?

Will they find out about Eden and pry into her life as well?

I don't know how they didn't dig up our past last time, and I can't guarantee they'll leave her alone this time.

And that doesn't sit well with me.

With a sigh, I check the crossroads and find it all clear.

But just as I put my foot on the gas, I notice something white moving fast toward the passenger side of the truck.

Eden reaches over and lays a hand on my forearm. "You know, I was thinking. Maybe after the event we could spend some—"

For the second time in my life, I see the world move in slow motion.

And yet everything happens so fast.

The turn of Eden's head toward the blur of white, her scream, the crunch of metal colliding, the screech of tires.

It seems like an eternity passes before I apply the brakes, for the truck to stop, the impact of the crash.

And then spinning until the back end of the truck hits a power pole and comes to a stop.

Then the quiet.

The eerie quiet.

It's as though I'm watching a crash on TV with the sound on mute.

Then suddenly the sound comes back on at full volume.

All at once, I hear the hiss of the truck engine, the incessant thump of the windshield wiper blades against the glass, the pounding of the rain on the roof of the cab.

The smell of rubber and antifreeze permeates the air.

Breathing hard, I unclench my hands from the wheel and look over at Eden.

She looks back at me, her chest heaving, her eyes wide.

But she's alive and breathing.

I unhook my seat belt and climb across the seat, patting her body, checking for injuries. "Are you okay?"

She nods slowly, her eyes still wide with shock. "Yeah, I think so."

When she turns her head, blood is running down the side of her face. "Fuck, Eden, your head's bleeding."

She lifts her hand slowly to her head. "I guess it does hurt a little bit."

A knock on her side window startles us both. I reach over and hit the down button to lower the window. Sheriff Youngblood is on the other side.

"You guys okay?"

"She's got a cut on her head, maybe a concussion."

I look down at Eden's face, which in just a couple of seconds' time has gone white as a ghost. "Eden? Are you okay? Talk to me."

"My foot. My head. Pain."

I shift to get a better look at the floorboard and see the side of the truck has caved in on impact, and her foot is trapped in a ridge of metal.

And there's blood.

Shit.

"Sheriff, we're going to need an ambulance and the fire department. It looks like her foot is caught."

"Already called for one. Looks like Stan Truman had a heart attack at the wheel."

He pats Eden's shoulder. "Take deep breaths and hang tight, ma'am. Medical help will be here shortly. Any other injuries?"

We're able to see Eden has no other visible injuries other than her foot and head.

But for me, that's two injuries too many.

As the sheriff jogs away to meet the fire department, Eden drops her head back and lets out a breath. A grim smile plays on her lips. "Guess I should have listened to you and stayed home, huh?"

"Sunshine..."

The fact Eden has injuries at all makes me want to be sick.

Before I can dwell on the fact that I've once again fucked up where she's concerned, the fire department descends on the truck.

When the sounds of the cutter hit the metal, I know they're having to cut Eden out. I can't hold off the nausea, and I run to the grass on the side of the road and vomit.

A small towel appears in front of me when I finish dry heaving.

"You alright?" Youngblood asks.

I take the towel and wipe my mouth. "Yeah, I'm fine."

"She's alert and they freed her from the truck. And she's in good hands now."

Red and blue lights fight against the gray skies to paint the air around us.

Youngblood watches me a moment. "You sure you're okay?"

"Yep."

The sheriff looks over to the white car that's facing the wrong direction in the middle of the road.

Another ambulance sits on the far side of the intersection, and one of the EMS workers shuts the back doors and hustles to the driver's side door.

I rub the back of my neck, tension lodged there that doesn't want to let up.

I'm pissed off that Eden's hurt and worried about the older man I know from the bait store.

He is a good man, a salt of the earth type.

"Fucking hell. Is he going to be okay?"

"Don't know yet." He pauses. "I'll make sure your truck is towed away and get the info for you."

"Thanks."

I look over at my truck that has finally quit smoking, the front end a mangled mess of steel, especially after they cut into the front fender to free Eden.

With a sigh, I look over at old man Stan's car, which is an older model sedan and will no doubt be totaled.

It's a blip on the radar for me to buy a brand-new truck, but that isn't the case for most of the full time locals on the island, and Stan is one of those people.

Fuck.

With my hands on my hips, I look at the wet ground. "You know, it was an accident. If you can let it ride, let it ride."

He nods and makes a note on his pad.

"And send old man Stan's tow bill to me. I'll take care of it."

"You're a saint, Hanover."

I scoff. "Yeah, yeah. Whatever."

He rolls his eyes and gestures toward the ambulance. "Take care of your girl. She's going to need it. And get some rest. You're both going to be sore as hell tomorrow."

"Thanks, man. Keep me posted on Stan."

"Will do," Youngblood says with a nod.

I jog over to the back of the ambulance where they have Eden on a gurney.

Eden's face is pale, her head lolled to one side, her eyes closed.

"Hey, Chase."

"Hey, Jack. How's she doing?"

"She's got a concussion," he says. "Nothing's broken, deep laceration on the leg that we'll stitch up. But we'll take her in to get a CT and observe her just to make sure there's not internal injuries."

I swallow back bile when he mentions *internal injuries.*

Dear God, please don't let there be anything we can't see. If I lose her, I won't survive.

"Are you coming, Chase?"

Jack's in the back of the ambulance, having already loaded Eden up, waiting for me expectantly.

"Yeah, I'm coming."

I climb up into the back and Jack shuts the doors behind me. Within minutes we're pulling into the small hospital on the island.

Fortunately, it's a quiet night with only one other person waiting in the emergency room, so Eden is taken right in.

They let me sit with her in the triage room, where she's awake but still hasn't said anything.

It's unnerving for her to be so quiet.

The nurse comes in and takes her vitals, then gives her an IV before asking for details on what brought her in. I fill in the gaps where Eden misses details.

When we're left alone, she leans her head back on the bed and turns toward me. A goofy smile plays on her lips. "Hey."

I smile at her. "Hey. How's the head?"

She rubs at her forehead, wincing slightly. "It hurts. But it's better than it was before. I must have been dehydrated. I'm feeling better since they put in the IV."

I chuckle. "Well, there's also some painkiller in that IV."

"Oh." Her eyes widen comically. "That's why I feel so good."

She squints an eye. "You know what? You're really handsome. Like, really handsome."

I bite back a laugh. "Thank you. You're really pretty."

"Thank you," she says, preening.

She leans to the side, precariously close to the edge of the bed.

I brace to catch her in case she falls forward. "You know what else?" she stage-whispers.

"What?"

"I really like having sex with you. Can we do it again?"

High Eden is hilarious.

Before I can answer, there's a knock on the door, and an older gentleman in scrubs and a lab coat walks in.

"Hey, look, it's the doctor!" she exclaims and claps her hands before leaning back on her pillow.

The doctor chuckles and introduces himself, then proceeds to ask several questions while examining her cuts, bumps, and bruises.

"I'm ordering a head CT to check the concussion, but it appears to be a light one. The nurse will be in shortly to take you for the scan. How's your pain right now? One being no pain, ten being the worst pain."

Eden wrinkles her nose. "I would say something like a four. Maybe. I don't know. I'm not really feeling any pain, but my handsome boyfriend here said they gave me some painkillers."

Boyfriend?

Warmth courses through my body, hearing her words. I know I already think of her as mine even when she isn't around, and to hear her say the same elates me.

"Hmmm...I think it's a one."

Something about that makes her giggle, and she slaps a hand over her mouth. "I'm so sorry."

The doctor chuckles and makes a note on the tablet in his hand. "I'd say you're doing okay at the moment, Ms. Mitchell. I'll be back when I get your scan results."

Before I can ask her about the whole boyfriend comment, the nurse comes and takes Eden to get her scan done.

While she's gone, I call Nate.

"Hey, man, can you come pick me and Eden up from the hospital?"

"Is everything okay?"

"Yeah, we had an accident and Eden got banged up."

"Damn, I'm sorry."

"Yeah, she's fine though. Getting a CT right now, but we should be good to go after that."

"On my way."

"Thanks, man."

"Don't mention it."

I go back into the room and sit down with a groan. Bracing my elbows on my knees, I rub my hands up and down my face, my stomach hollow and achy.

What the fuck with my life?

I have more money than I can ever spend, all the material things a man can ask for.

But when it comes to people I love?

My life is a total shit show.

I sit here in a hospital, waiting for the woman I love to finish getting her head examined because of a car accident.

Another motherfucking car accident.

Except this time I was driving, which makes it even worse.

In the sensible part of my mind, I know it isn't my fault. It was a freak thing. How often does someone have a heart attack behind the wheel?

I should've been more insistent that she stay behind while I helped Stewie.

But the truth is I had wanted her with me, not left back at the house, so it had been easy for her to convince me otherwise.

Me and my motherfucking selfish ways.

My father had been right all along.

I'm a walking disaster, a selfish bastard who doesn't give two shits about anyone he really cares about.

It doesn't matter how many good deeds I do—in the end I'm still a selfish prick.

Always looking out for number one.

No, Eden didn't die. But she ended up with a concussion because of me.

All roads lead back to me and my fucked-up ways. The best thing I can do for her is to let her go.

Now I just need to remember this when I see her.

A few moments later, Eden's wheeled back in and can hardly keep her eyes open.

There will be no meaningful conversation tonight.

She snoozes while we wait for Nate, who arrives within the hour.

We get Eden loaded up and she goes back to sleep in the front seat. It's a quiet ride to our end of the island.

"Looks like the power's been restored," Nate says, as we pull up to my gate.

"We were lucky this time."

"No kidding."

He pulls up to the front door. "Need any help?"

"No, we'll be fine."

He eyes me over his shoulder. "How are *you*?"

I look out the side window. "I'm good."

"You sure about that?"

I meet his eyes. "Positive. I'm not worried about me right now. I need to get Eden inside and settled. I'll worry about me later."

Nate sighs. "Okay, fine. Do you need any help?"

"Just get the doors for me." I toss him my keys to open the front door.

Minutes later, Nate has left and I've settled Eden into bed.

The nurse told me signs I need to look for from Eden overnight, things I already knew from the time a ball bounced off the mound wrong and knocked my ass out.

It was the only time I'd ever missed a start, and I'd had a headache for days.

After setting her pain meds and a bottle of water on the nightstand, I squat down beside the bed, studying her.

The soft curves of her face are etched in my mind.

The way her lashes brush the top of her cheekbones makes her seem almost angelic.

With a quivering hand, I brush back some strands that escaped her ponytail as she murmurs something under her breath I can't decipher.

The pain in my chest aches like a bitch.

It's like someone has reached in and pulled out my heart while it's still beating.

The need to move is overwhelming, so I stand and leave her to rest.

In the living room, I head for the liquor cabinet, pouring two fingers of whiskey and throwing it back.

The burn of the whiskey replaces the churning in my gut.

I don't want to let her leave again. But my selfish ways will always end up being an issue where she'll end up hurt.

And for once in my life, I'm thinking about someone other than me.

A sudden rage comes over me and I throw the glass against the wall, shattering it into a shower of tiny pieces.

I know what I have to do and it kills me.

Cutting ties is the only thing I can do to show her how much I love her.

I have to let her go.

TWENTY
eden

I BLINK against the pain that feels like a marching band is practicing inside my skull.

I put a hand to my head, and my fingertips brush against what feels like a bandage on my forehead.

"Good morning."

I open my eyes and warily lift my head.

When it seems like I can sit all the way up without losing the contents of my stomach, I look around the dimly lit room. "Chase?"

"I'm here."

"Where am I? What's going on?"

He sits next to me, his weight shifting the bed and making my stomach momentarily lurch. "You're in my bed. You've been out for a while. Want some water?"

When nodding my head proves to be painful, I croak out a yes.

After he gives me water, his eyes search my face as though looking for something. "Do you remember the car accident?"

I think back to the last thing I can remember before now.

"Um, I remember going to help Stewie. Then we were headed back here..."

That's when everything goes fuzzy, and I'm unable to remember much after that.

Though it seems like there is a memory of screaming and a jolt to my body that's just beyond my reach of remembering.

But there's something pushing at my memory.

Something that's important, that I need to remember, but I can't reach it. "That's all I can remember."

"We were hit by a car that ran a stop sign. The driver had a heart attack and lost control of his car. You suffered a concussion, a gash just above the ankle that needed stitches, and some bruising."

That's why my body feels like I've been beaten like a steak being tenderized with a meat hammer. "Wow. Okay. Well, no wonder I hurt all over. And why my foot hurts so much."

"Yeah, it was trapped in between some metal that had caved in. No broken bones though, which is nothing short of a miracle, to be honest."

I rub my bandaged temple. "That's good at least. How's the other driver?"

Chase's mouth presses together in a firm line. "They stabilized him long enough to get him to the hospital, but he died on the operating table."

"Oh my God. Did you know him?"

He nods. "Yeah, he owned the bait store in town."

"I'm so sorry, Chase."

"Shitty all the way around."

"Yeah." I sigh and look around the room. "What time is it? It's so dark in here."

"It's about eleven."

"In the morning?"

"Yeah."

"Well, I guess that's one way to get some extra sleep. I haven't slept for ten hours or so in...well, I can't remember how long."

"Um, Eden. You've been out for two days."

My mouth drops open. "What? I slept for two days?"

He nods. "You don't remember waking up a few times when I helped you to the bathroom?"

In my shocked haze, I dimly recall Chase walking me to the bathroom, but I thought it was a dream. "I thought I was dreaming."

"No, it really happened."

He pulls my phone out of his pocket. "You should be able to look at a screen now without too much of a headache. A woman named Katie is blowing up your phone, so I answered it yesterday and let her know what's going on. She said to call her when you could and that she had everything covered."

"Thank you."

I reach out gingerly and take the phone from him.

He's careful not to touch me. In fact, I just realized that he sat next to me, but only close enough to give me the water. He's careful not to touch me or get too close.

I study his posture, and for the first time since I woke up, I notice his body is tense and he looks ready to bolt.

What's happened the last two days while I was out cold?

"Chase, what's going on?"

"What do you mean?"

What *do* I mean?

I can't really put it into words.

All I know is that the Chase I spent time with before the accident is not the same man in front of me now.

This is the Chase I saw when I first arrived on the island a few days ago.

Has it only been a few days ago? A helluva lot has changed in such a short period of time.

When I don't say anything more, he stands, shoving his hands into his pockets. "I've got some things to do. If you need me, just shoot me a text."

"Chase, wait a minute." I swing my legs over to the side of the bed, and when the room stops moving, I stand and face him. "What's going on with you?"

He crosses his arms over his chest. "There's nothing going on with me."

His flat, unemotional tone matches the stony mask on his face.

It's like I don't know him at all.

I stare into his eyes, searching for something, anything, that would show me the real Chase.

The Chase I know, the Chase that I know without a doubt I'm still in love with all these years later.

"Why are you shutting me out?"

He sighs and looks away. "I'm not shutting you out, Eden. I'm just doing what I should have done since you got here."

"And what's that?"

"Not get too close to you."

"Chase, we have history. I'm not sure we could have avoided it if we tried."

"Yeah, well, I should have tried harder. Things would have been different if I hadn't let you in again."

I rub at my forehead, where I clash with the fabric reminder of the accident. The pain makes me wince involuntarily.

His eyes narrow on the action, and he frowns. He waves a hand toward me. "See what I mean?"

"No, I don't follow you at all."

God, my head throbs. At this point, I'm not sure if it's my

concussion or his train of thought. I'm trying to follow his line of reasoning, but it makes no sense to me.

He sighs and walks closer to me. "Eden, all I know how to do is hurt people. Everything I touch turns to shit."

I shake my head slowly. "That's not true, Chase. You were one of major league baseball's best pitchers. You've gone into history books. Your name will be known for years to come. Little boys want to grow up to be like you."

"Fuck that." He runs a hand through his hair. "Fine, when it comes to baseball, I was the Golden Boy. But when it comes to relationships? I always fuck it up somehow."

He paces the floor like a caged tiger on the prowl. "It's like I used up all my luck on the diamond. You know this, Eden."

With a pause, he looks at me, his eyes full of anguish. "It's why you should be running the other way. Not standing here trying to convince me I'm something I'm not."

"I'm standing here trying to convince you because that's not what I see."

He laughs without humor. "Are you kidding me right now? How do you not see me for what I am? You're one of the people I've hurt the most, Eden. I was too selfish to be there for you when you needed me. I chose my baseball career over you."

"But I told you to go! It was my decision and my choice to stay with my mother."

He stops and looks over at me, shaking his head. "Eden, we both know you had no choice in that matter."

"There's always a choice. I stayed because my mother would have haunted me to the day I died if I'd left her while she was sick."

Something in my chest twists and I go to stand in front of him. "Did I want you to go? No, but that was the choice that I made. Can't you see that what I did to you was the same thing?

I put my needs ahead of yours. You're not to blame for all that, Chase."

His jaw bunches and his cheek tics. "It isn't the same thing. You stayed because you needed to take care of your mother. That's what kids do. It's admirable. It was selfless because that's who you are."

His face softens as he reaches out and cups my cheek. "You're one of the best people I know, Eden. Smart, ambitious, beautiful, and selfless. Is it any wonder that I've loved you since I met you in English lit?"

My heart stops. "You never told me that."

He nods, but the look in his eyes is sad, resigned. "I realized it soon after we met. I thought it was just lust, you know? But after we slept together that first time, I knew without a doubt that I was stupid in love with you."

Dropping his hand from my face, he looks away. "I tried to convince myself over the years after we broke up that it was just a college thing. We were young. It would have never worked once we graduated."

He starts to pace again, running a hand through his hair. All I can do is stand and watch him, my heart aching.

"But no matter where I was, what I did, you never left me. You were always on my mind. No matter who I met, no matter how many women I had. It was just a temporary respite from thoughts of you. Even with Heather, I knew it wouldn't last. I knew better and I still did it."

He stalks over to me and holds my shoulders. "Can't you see it, Eden? I chose me every time. I did it with my mother, I did it with you, and I did it with Heather. You deserve so much better than what I can give you, than what I'll eventually do to you. We both know it."

I cup his face with my hands. "Chase, I'm willing to try this again. With you. I want us to be together. You deserve love too, Chase."

He steps back and looks at me with cold eyes again. "No. I don't deserve it. I never have. My father was right. What kind of person deserves love when all they think about is what they want in life? If I hadn't defied my parents' rules, my mother would still be alive. If I hadn't married Heather knowing I didn't really love her, we never would have been in that car and she'd still be alive. Her family would still have her. If I didn't have such a need for you, you wouldn't have a concussion right now."

His voice breaks on the last word.

But his eyes are steady on mine, and what I see there shatters my heart. He really does think he's a hopeless case.

The one thing that will help him is the one thing he won't do.

"Chase, those things weren't your fault." I step toward him. "Don't give up on us."

He stares at me for several seconds, his hands jammed on his hips.

Those green eyes hold shadows and secrets that I can only guess at right now. But after a few moments, they harden and turn cold.

Without an answer, he goes over to the windows and opens the room-darkening shades.

It isn't a sunny day, but the storm clouds are gone, and the wind has died down to a mere sea breeze.

He turns back to me.

"You can go home now, Eden. The bridge is open, and Katie has your new flight scheduled for tomorrow."

I open and close my mouth in shock. Then his words register fully. "You called Katie? You want me out of here that bad?"

"You can get back to New York and your business."

"That's not fair, Chase."

His eyes narrow on me. "So, you're telling me that you came here to reconcile with me? To tell me why you ran out and didn't speak to me for four years? Didn't return my calls?"

I open my mouth, but he holds up a hand. "Don't bother, Mitchell. Tit for tat. I left you, you left me. Now we're even. Right?"

Tears fill my eyes and my vision blurs. "No, I—"

"You what, Eden?" He lifts his arms out to his side. "You only came here to get something from me. Am I wrong?"

I swallow, panic clawing at my throat. "No, you're not wrong. But all it took was spending time with you to remember what I was missing. And that's you, Chase."

He shakes his head and looks at the floor for a moment before looking back at me. "This was just sex, Eden. Remember? All we do is hurt each other. You deserve so much better than what I can give you."

My stomach drops to my feet, and my head is light. "But I love you."

"I love you too. I've never stopped loving you. But it isn't enough." He shakes his head. "It just isn't enough."

I wipe the tears rolling down my cheeks with a hard swipe. "Fine. You want me gone, I'll go."

Anger and desperation grabs hold of me and I poke him in the chest. "I know what this is, Chase, and you're wrong. Love is enough; you're just too scared to see it. Too blinded by fear and some misguided notion that your father planted in your head and poisoned you with when you were still a kid. And it makes me sad for you."

I straighten my shoulders. "I love you, but I won't wait for you. I won't keep putting myself out there for you. Yes, I ran four years ago because I didn't want you to hurt me. And yes, I came here with only one thing in mind—to secure you as a speaker."

Stepping back, I clear my throat. "There's something here between us that no matter what has happened, doesn't go away."

I pause, waiting to see if anything I've said has gotten through to him. He stares at me for a beat.

"Charley offered to give you a ride to Jacksonville whenever you're ready."

It's my turn to laugh without humor. "Well, you worked this all out while I slept, didn't you? Wow. You're right, Chase. You are a real bastard."

He lifts his arms out to his side. "I told you what I was, Eden. You're just finally seeing me for who I am."

I nod slowly and pick up my phone. "Yeah. Well, I'll get packed then."

He nods and leaves the room, closing the door quietly behind him and effectively shutting down anything we'd ever had.

But if that's how he wants it, I'll go.

He may have just destroyed me, ripped my heart out of my chest and stomped it bloody, but I have my dignity, damn it.

It might be all I have but I have it.

The tears don't fall while I throw clothes in my carry-on bag.

I dress in my armor of a pencil skirt and button-down blouse —except for my heels given my injury—a teeny tiny amount of confidence warming me as I slide into my own clothes again.

But it isn't much.

Not enough for me to get back to where I was before.

I toss my toiletries into the bag and zip it all up.

No turning back now.

I call Charley to let her know I'm ready to get the fuck out of dodge.

On the end of the bed, I lay the T-shirt Chase gave me the morning after we'd had what, for me anyway, had been soul-defining sex.

I thought we had a real connection again. A stronger one than we'd ever had before.

But the joke's on me.

He says he loves me, even acts like it at times, but it has all been a ruse.

I run my fingertips over the soft fabric before pulling back. Burning it or ripping it at the seams crosses my mind.

But I'm Eden Mitchell. I don't do those sorts of things.

I have a business to run. A life to get back to in the greatest city in the world.

If Cape Sands has taught me anything, it's that I have all I need back in the city.

I don't need a man, and I don't need relaxation. I need the vibe of the city and I need my business.

When I'm finished packing, I head out to the living room, finding Chase in the foyer. He's leaning against the wall, his head down, but he looks up when I walk into the room.

He straightens to his full height and holds out his hand. My heart leaps in hope for a moment until he speaks.

"If you give me your keys, I'll take care of your rental for you."

"Oh gee, thanks." I dig through my purse, anger biting at me like an angry dog. "You know what? You're right."

When I find the keys, I toss them to him. He catches them against his chest, but doesn't say anything.

"You *are* totally fucked-up, Chase. And all I can say to that is good riddance."

His expression is blank and he doesn't say a word to me as I open the front door and slam it behind me.

I'm closing the door on my past and leaving it here.

And maybe I'm leaving my heart and soul behind, but other than that, there's nothing else for me here.

Charley pulls up a few moments later, and after stowing my carry-on in the back seat of her SUV, I slide into the front seat and send her a smile. "Thanks for taking me. I appreciate it."

"It's no problem. I'm happy to help." She pulls away from the house, and I lean back against the seat.

Even driving away, Chase has a pull on me because I do the one thing I shouldn't have.

I look back.

Chase stands on the front porch, watching us drive away.

And I promptly burst into tears.

TWENTY-ONE
chase

"GIMME ANOTHER, AL."

Al raises a bushy gray brow and leans on the bar, the requisite bartender towel draped over his shoulder. "How you gettin' home, Hanover?"

"Home"—I point at him—"is a crock of shit. You mark my words."

Nonplussed, Al says again, "How you gettin' home, Hanover?"

I glare at him and dig my keys out of my pocket, tossing them on the bar. They clatter loudly on the well-worn, wood bar.

"There. Happy? Now, give me another Jameson. Double this time. And another beer."

"I'll get you a ride." Al swipes my keys, not bothered by my little temper tantrum.

"Whatever. Where's my drink?"

Al shakes his head and turns away. I'm a grumpy bastard most of the time, without having the reasons I do tonight.

Tonight, I'm just a straight-up prick, even to Al, whom I'm nice to any other time.

I've been a surly shithead to every soul unfortunate enough to cross my path since Eden left.

It's been three days since she walked out.

But this time, I pushed her away.

That's right folks, I got her before she could get me.

Too bad my whole motherfucking body hurts with a pain that seems immune to any type of painkiller.

The first two days, I spent inside a bottle at home. Linda had shown up, ready to clean up and do the job I pay her to do.

But when she tried to strip the sheets on my bed to wash, I yelled at her not to touch a fucking thing and sent her home.

I'm not ready for the scent of Eden to be cleared away. It's all I have left.

It's all I deserve.

When I woke up this morning, a.k.a. day three of purgatory, hung over like a motherfucker, shame spread through me for yelling at Linda yesterday.

I sent her a text, apologizing and giving her another week off with pay. I'm grateful she forgave me, but her messages conveyed how concerned she is about me.

I don't need her concern. I just need time to work Eden out of my system.

After cleaning up the pigsty formerly known as my living room, I showered, dressed, and made my sorry ass be productive.

Regardless of what went down, I have a life to live, things to straighten out.

I called the insurance company, bought a new truck online, and stopped at the local funeral home and paid the tab for Stan's funeral, then went to the florist and sent a large arrangement to his family.

The accident might have been his fault, but it had been just that—an accident. The family had lost their husband, father, brother. This time, my losses had been superficial.

Stan had sunk every dime they had into his shop, and while he did a good business, I also knew the family didn't have much in the way of extra money to pay for a funeral. And life insurance took forever to come through.

It's a fact I know well.

Since it'll be a few days before my new truck is delivered, I extended the rental on Eden's SUV and paid it in full.

That pain-in-the-ass little voice in my head likes to mock the masochist I am, telling me I only kept her rental so I could smell her perfume.

Little fucker.

I drove around, surveying the damage on the island, and decided to check on my properties.

Something I should have already done. Thankfully, they all came out unscathed, except for some tree debris in the yards.

Several times along my drive, I stopped and helped out where it was needed.

Anything to keep me busy, away from the house, and thinking about *her*.

I'd worked so hard to build a fortress around myself, and Eden had waltzed in, wearing her four-hundred-dollar heels, and torn the walls down in just seventy-two hours.

Everywhere I look in my house I'm reminded of her.

Shit, I may have to move.

All in all, my day had been productive, but I didn't feel any better.

After helping the high school baseball team clean up the field, I decided to head to Al's for one drink to take the edge off before I go home.

I tried to stay straight for a night but the thought of going back home?

I can't bear it.

Which is how I'm now drunk being a piece-of-shit customer to Al, who just placed a double shot and beer in front of me with a click on the wood.

I toss the whiskey back and hiss at the burn. It lands in my belly alongside the other shots I've had, but I'm beginning to get to the point where I no longer feel the comforting warmth spread through me like the first ones had.

How many have I had?

I try to count on my fingers, but I keep losing count when I get to three and have to start over.

"You're on number five. But this one was a double so it's more like seven."

Nate appears on the stool beside me like he's a fucking magician or something. I look around, my whiskey-and-beer-addled brain confused.

"Where'd the hell you come from? The wall?"

"Al called me to give you a ride." Nate nods at Al. "Just a Coke for me."

"Give me a ride. I don't need a fucking ride," I mutter under my breath. "What I need is a lobotomy."

I squint over at him when Al slides the soda in front of Nate. "You come to a bar to get a Coke?"

He shrugs. "Not usually, but someone has to drive your sorry ass home."

I shake my head. "Whatever, dude," I grumble, sipping my beer.

"So...want to talk about it?"

"Not really."

"Okay, that's cool." He sips his soda.

Christ, why the hell doesn't he drink a beer with me?

I squint at him again. "You know what? I don't like you."

He just grins. "Well, now that's too bad. I'm pretty fond of your grumpy ass."

"No, I mean it." I swallow another swig of beer and start back in on him. "You got it freaking all, man. A woman that loves you, a family. And your career didn't end in disgrace.."

"True. But that's just one part of you. You can have the woman and the family too. We aren't all that different in that area."

I shake my head. "Oh no. We're totally different. You have the woman you want."

Holding up a finger, swaying slightly, I continue. "And you're a fucking model for sports clothes. I mean, seriously?"

Nate leans back and gives me the side-eye.

I think.

In my inebriated state, it's a little hard to tell what he's doing. "You could have the woman too if you'd get your head out of your ass. You know, a lot of guys would give their left and right nuts to be sitting where you are right now."

"You mean a lonely drunk guy in a bar?"

He rolls his eyes at me. "No, dumbass. I mean,"—he leans forward on the bar and drops his voice like he's telling me a secret—"you're a baseball legend. You've broken long-standing records. You have multiple houses, cars, every toy known to man."

I scoff. "Those are just things."

"Exactly. Don't forget all the good you do here. You donated money to repair baseball fields. You've paid for the high school baseball team to get new uniforms. You give your time to them and your money whenever they need it. People around here love your grumpy ass."

"They wouldn't if they knew me."

Nate's brow furrows. "What do you mean if they knew you?"

I drain the last of my beer and signal for another one. Al purses his lips but pops the top off another amber bottle. "Last one, Hanover."

I wave him away. I point at Al's retreating back with my thumb. "Think Al loves me?"

Nate chuckles. "Maybe not this very moment, but it's only because you're being a dick on purpose."

He stares at me as though waiting for me to spill my guts. When a few moments pass and I don't say anything, he says, "So what do you mean, if they knew you?"

I sigh and rub my hands down my face. "Look, I'm toxic, okay? When I was fourteen, my mother died. Want to know how?"

"How?"

"From the flu. She had an undiagnosed rare lung condition. Her body couldn't recover from the virus."

"I'm sorry to hear that."

"Guess who gave it to her?" I ask, ignoring his platitudes, and point to myself. "This punk, right here."

I raise my voice and stand in a theatrical way. "Yes, ladies and gentlemen, Chase 'Hollywood Golden Boy' Hanover, selfish bastard extraordinaire, decided to go to a party I wasn't supposed to go to. And guess what parting gift I left with that night?"

I point at Nate. "Would you like to guess, my friend?"

Cupping my ear like I'm waiting to hear his response, I give him a go-ahead motion, but he just stares at me with a bland look.

I take that as permission to move on and plow ahead. "Ding, ding! That's right. The flu! And she did what mothers are supposed to do and took care of me. And then want to know what we did a couple of weeks later? We buried her."

I sway on my feet until I sit with a thump on the stool.

Bitterness stings my tongue and I stop talking, unable to swallow around the knot in my throat. I can still hear my father yelling at me, accusing me of being a selfish little bastard who only thought of himself.

I clear my throat, trying to continue, but I have no more theatrics for this part of the story. "My father accused me of getting her sick and killing her. He never looked at me the same after that."

Rolling my lips in to hold back any sort of emotion, I pause. "Could be because he stayed drunk after that until he died. He lived just long enough for my little brother to graduate from high school. Then when little bro went off to the military, Dad drank himself to the grave."

"That's a shitty deal, man. And I understand shitty deals."

I wave a hand, not wanting the pity. It's why I never tell anyone my story. "What's done is done."

Nate sips his soda. "That's true." He shifts on the stool. "But do you really believe you killed your mom? If she had this rare condition, she could have died from it some other way. And who says it was you who gave her the flu?"

"What do you mean?"

"Did she not ever leave the house?"

My brows furrow. "Of course she did. She volunteered all over town, with the kids, in the hospital."

"And you think you're the only way she could have gotten sick?" Nate asks.

"I—" My mouth snaps shut. "My father always said it was me who made her sick. Me who killed her. That's the way it happened."

Right?

It had to be.

My father hadn't been father of the year being an alcoholic

and all, but he still did things with us at times, and he never physically abused any of us.

"But what if it wasn't?" he asks.

"Why would he tell me I was the cause of killing my mother?"

I rub my hands over my head and down my face.

Nate sighs. "I don't know. And since he's dead, his reasoning went with him. But if I had to guess? I'd guess it was because he was helpless and needed someone to blame."

"Yeah, well, fuck him."

Nate's quiet for a moment. "Why do I feel like that's not the only thing?"

"Because you're also smart. There was Eden. I chose my baseball career over her. She needed me when her mother was sick. And I left." I throw my hands up in the air. "Just left. Got mad at her for staying behind. I mean, what kind of prick does that?"

"A young one with his head up his ass?"

Nodding, I drink my beer, sloshing some of it around in my mouth. "Exactly. Guys like me. I do that." I rub at my chin with the back of my hand. "And then there's Heather."

I look around surreptitiously, half waiting for some paps to jump out at me like they used to when the topic of Heather arose.

"I know I heard a few things about that, but I also know how these rags work. Want to tell me what really went down?"

I sigh and lay my forehead on the bar for a moment, enjoying the cool, smooth surface against my skin, before lifting up again and almost falling backward off my stool.

"Long, long, long story short. Between the video of me fighting with Ty, Heather's family suing me—even though it was thrown out of court—plus all the lies Ty and her family spouted to whoever would listen, the media had a field day participating in the downfall of me and my reputation. The story got twisted to make it sound like I caused the crash."

"But I didn't think you were the one driving."

I shake my head, and the room tilts around me a bit. "I wasn't. Heather was."

"Then...why do they think you caused it?"

I sigh. "I made the mistake of trusting her family and told them the details when they asked for them. We'd been arguing just before it happened. She'd told me she was pregnant. And it wasn't mine. It was Ty's. She wanted a divorce."

His eyes widen. "Holy shit."

I nod so much I think my head might roll off my shoulders. I point a finger at him. "Yep. See why your life is better than mine? And don't forget, your heart and body isn't owned by a fucking woman you can't have because you and Charley made it work."

Eden's face pops into my brain and the world spins around me.

As I start to fall off the stool, Nate comes up underneath my shoulder and props me up. "Come on, Chase. I'll take you home."

I pat his shoulder—at least I think I do. "You're a gurd friend, dude."

For some reason, I start laughing. Nate half drags, half walks me to his truck and pours me into the passenger seat.

The last thing I remember is the image of Eden swimming in my mind before everything goes black.

TWENTY-TWO

chase

SOMETHING cold and wet hits my shoulder.

Annoyed, I grunt and swipe at it to make it go away.

There's a tiny growl just before a swat of needle pricks hits my face.

"What the fuck?"

Where the hell am I?

In spite of the little drummer boy playing a rocking drum solo in my skull, I crack open an eyelid and slam it back shut with a moan when light pours in, causing my stomach to lurch.

Son of a bitch. What the fuck did I do last night?

A tiny mewl rings in my ear before something soft lies under my chin.

"Looks like she likes you. I can't understand why though."

I jump when I hear Lucas's voice.

"Jesus, do you ever make any noise when you move?"

I slowly open my eyes again, and my vision is full of gray fur. "What is on me?"

He chuckles and the ball of fur is lifted away. "A kitten."

When I don't feel like I'm going to lose the contents of my stomach, I turn my head to survey my surroundings.

Laid out on a sofa, there's a blanket draped over me and I'm still in my clothes from the night before.

A large flat-screen TV takes up one wall, and the rest of the room is so tidy, it looks like it's hardly ever used.

"I'd start with the water first."

On the coffee table next to me is a cup of steaming coffee and a bottle of water.

I lean my head back to find Lucas sitting on the loveseat, the gray-and-white kitten now in his lap.

With a sigh and a surge of mortification setting in, I slowly sit up and swing my legs to the side.

Elbows on my knees, I hold my aching head in my hands for a moment before looking up at him.

"Thanks," I say, reaching for the bottle of water.

It's an effort I don't have the energy for, but I manage to keep from chugging the bottle to relieve the foul-tasting ball of cotton that has grown in my mouth overnight.

From the corner of my eye, Lucas watches me, sipping his coffee, his eyes calm and understanding.

The little fur ball jumps over the blanket and picks her way across the sofa, plopping down next to me.

I run a hand over her soft fur, which makes her seem bigger than she is, and she tries to bite my fingers.

"Where did she come from?"

"I found the kittens this morning. They were stuck under some palm fronds in the yard."

"By themselves?"

He nods. "There were three of them, and it looked like maybe mama left and didn't get back."

As if I need another thing to pull at my fucking heartstrings. "Where are the other two?"

"Odette took them. I'm just keeping her until I find her a home."

"Good ol' Odette."

"Yep." He pauses, watching me pet the cat and sip my coffee. "Better?"

"Yeah." I run a hand through my disheveled hair. "How did I end up at your place?"

"Nate was going to take you to his, but Lucy was having a rough night and Charley needed help. So he brought you here."

"Shit. I feel like I should apologize to you and Charley and Nate."

"Al too. He said you'd been a real asshole."

I sigh heavily and lean my head back. "Why didn't you just take me home?"

"When you started talking a lot of nonsense, it made me nervous. Add to the fact that there was one point that you couldn't stop throwing up for a while."

I drop my head to my hand. "Oh my God. I'm so sorry."

"Seriously, man. Don't worry about it. Friends take care of friends. Even if they do accuse the other of wanting to sleep with his girl. And it seems like you could use a friend right now."

I groan and cover my face. "Fuck, man. You should have punched my ass out."

He shrugs a shoulder. "I thought about it, but it wasn't worth the pain my hand would endure hitting your stubborn face."

I swallow another swig of water and look out the glass sliders of Lucas's living room. A huge balcony overlooks the beach and the Atlantic beyond.

There's a void in me right now that feels like all the water in ocean can't fill.

My throat burns from vomiting my insides out the night before. At least that's what I'm telling myself.

It has nothing to do with the fact my eyes are watering.

"So, what are you going to do about Eden?"

I clear my throat, but can't meet his eyes. "I don't know. What did I say to you?"

"Nate and I compared notes this morning, and it seems you told us both all about your dad."

"Ah, fuck me."

"You rambled drunkenly all about how your father told you how worthless you were for 'killing your mother,' and how you'd let Eden down before by leaving her for baseball and how you don't want to hurt her again. And how all those things make you the worst person in the world. And you deserve to be alone."

When I finally meet his eyes, I see the bastard is challenging me. Challenging me to dispute him.

Because when he says it like that, it sounds a bit ridiculous and self-serving.

At least, that's what I'd think if someone had said it to me.

Still, it's how I feel. Isn't it? Or is that how I'd convinced myself to feel?

"Look,"—he leans forward, hands clasped between his knees—"I don't know what happened between you two. But I do know Eden cried the entire way to Jacksonville."

"Jesus, you and Nate are like two old gossipy women."

I run a hand into my hair, yanking on a handful of it. The one thing I hate is to make Eden cry.

He's unaffected by my insult. "Apparently, she told Charley a few things. The biggest thing being that she still loves you."

The fact that I laid bare all of my demons and all but kicked her out of my house yet she tells Charley she still loves me fills my chest with hope.

But it's quickly followed by the fact that I have no idea how to fix this.

Especially since I'm the asshole that pushed her away.

Blowing out a long breath, I pick up the kitten and bring her up to look her in the eye. "I fucked up good, didn't I?"

She sniffs the tip of my nose and then lets out a tiny mewl.

With a sigh, I set the furball on the sofa next to me and look over at Lucas. "What would you do in my shoes?"

His sigh is heavy. "Shit, man. Love is complicated for guys like us. We travel all the time, the sport consumes us, and the media is always up in our business. Not to mention, neither one of us had a very good upbringing."

He sips his coffee. "I know you don't want to hear this, but Eden is the type of woman I'd love to have by my side. Beautiful, smart, professional, well put together—"

That possessive caveman in me tries to come out and play, but I manage to keep him at bay. Well, sort of.

I glare at him and he raises a brow.

"Dude, why aren't you with Darcy?"

"Because it would be like kissing my sister. May I continue?"

I wave my hand in a go-ahead gesture.

"With a woman like that, you do whatever you have to in order to keep her. And if you have that chemistry? When you find one, you hold on and don't let go."

"I know. Fuck, I know. But the media—"

"Fuck the media, man. Are you going to let those fair-weather fuckers dictate your life forever? Look,"—he moves to the edge of the sofa—"the truth is, your career as a ballplayer is over."

I know he's right, but hearing it from him, hearing the reality of it even after a few years, hurts my chest.

He continues. "Which I'm sure is tough to hear, but here's the upside. Who cares what the media says anymore? It isn't like it's going to tank your career. And not being an active player anymore means they're usually looking for a guy who is and has screwed up somehow. That poor sucker is a bigger story than you these days."

I rub the cat's head, letting her purring soothe me.

Lucas's words sting but he isn't wrong.

"One more thing," he says. "No one here in Cape Sands believes any of that shit the media has said about you. You don't have to worry about sponsorships and money. So, what are you so worried about?"

He has a point. What *am* I worried about?

My father is dead. Heather's family has stayed out of the public eye since I paid them a healthy sum.

There's no one left to come out and call me a killer anymore.

And even if there is, like Nate says, I'm not tabloid news anymore.

Have I been so stuck in my past that I'm letting go of my future?

"I need to do the charity ball."

"Is that the event she asked you to help her with?"

I side-eye him. "How did you know about that?"

"The speaker thing? Charley."

"Of course." I sigh and rub the back of my neck, sweat a sheen on my skin. "I can do this, right?"

"Hell, yeah, you can. It all comes down to what you want. A life alone on the island or a life with the woman who will stand by you no matter what—heal your wounds."

He points at me. "Because I saw you guys together only once and that's all it took to see you two could light up the Eastern Seaboard with the chemistry. Plus, you may not know it, but you get this wistful look in your eyes when you look at her."

I scoff. "You're full of shit. I do not."

Do I?

"Whatever you say, man." He leans back, stretching an arm out across the back of the loveseat. "Listen, don't be like me, Hanover. Believe it or not, I wasn't always a playboy. I've only ever wanted one woman in my life. And I had the love of my life once. I fucked up big time and let her go. Evelyn was the best thing I ever had. But even with it right in front of me, I couldn't see through my own bullshit to keep her."

I'm stunned to hear the guy known for his bedroom prowess was once a one-woman man. "Where is she now?"

His sigh is heavy with sadness. "Last I knew, she's in Phoenix and married to a physical therapist."

If I found out Eden was married, I'd be gutted. "I'm sorry, man."

He shakes his head. "Neither here nor there, now. But you know what it's like to have that special woman who you want to fight the whole world for. Eden is special. Hold on to it with all you have."

He smirks. "If you don't go get her, I'm going to go to New York and get her myself."

My jaw muscles bunch and my eyes narrow.

With a snap, he points at me. "Gotcha."

I kick his foot. "You fucker."

He laughs and sips his coffee.

Staring out the windows to the ocean beyond, I absently scratch behind the kitten's ears.

No one ever told me life would be fair. Or that it would be easy.

And if I get my head out of my ass long enough to think about it, I've had a more than fair life.

Because shit happens. People die. Freak accidents occur.

The media loses interest and you can move on with your life.

Lucas is right.

Do I want to be alone in a big house and think of all that could have been?

Or do I want to live out my days with Eden—if she'll take me back—and build a life with her?

Isn't whatever time I have with her better than none at all?

The demon with my father's voice that I've lived with my whole life is kicking and screaming at me to be scared, to choose safety.

To not let anyone in because I'm not worth the trouble.

Baseball is the only thing I've ever been good at and even that has been taken from me.

Even if Eden tells me to go straight to hell without collecting two hundred dollars, I'll at least know the demon can no longer hold me bound to my past.

My heart surges with hope, and I stand so abruptly I almost drop the kitten. "I'm sorry, I need to go."

Lucas stands, a dubious look on his face. "You okay? Need a ride?"

"I'm good and no, I could use the walk to clear my head. It's just a couple of miles. I have a plan." I hand him the kitten. "Here's your cat."

He holds his hands up. "No way, she's yours now."

When I cuddle the little thing against my chest, she crawls up and settles into the crook of my neck.

I chuckle. "Yeah, I guess so. Hey, man. Thank you."

"For what?"

"For everything. For putting me up last night, for not kicking my ass even though I'm sure I deserved it."

He simply nods once. "Get the hell out of here and go get your girl."

We do the one arm bro-hug thing and I leave, walking along the beachfront road that will lead to my house.

"Well, I didn't expect to come home with a cat, but here we are. You just need a name."

When I get home, my head is clear and my plan is solid.

Step one. Call my agent.

"Liz Fallon."

"Liz? It's Chase."

"Well, well. Nice to hear from the Golden Boy."

Her voice is both welcoming and fear-inducing for me. Under that snarky tone, she's glad I called.

Lord knows she bothered me enough.

"Yeah. Listen, I need your help." I blow out a breath. "I'm ready."

I don't need to tell her more.

She knows exactly what I mean. By the tone of her voice, she has that feline ready-to-take-on-the-world smile on her face. The one no one wants to see from the other side of the negotiating table.

It's part of the reason I hired her.

Maybe I should name my cat Liz.

"It's about damn time, Hanover. What you got in mind?"

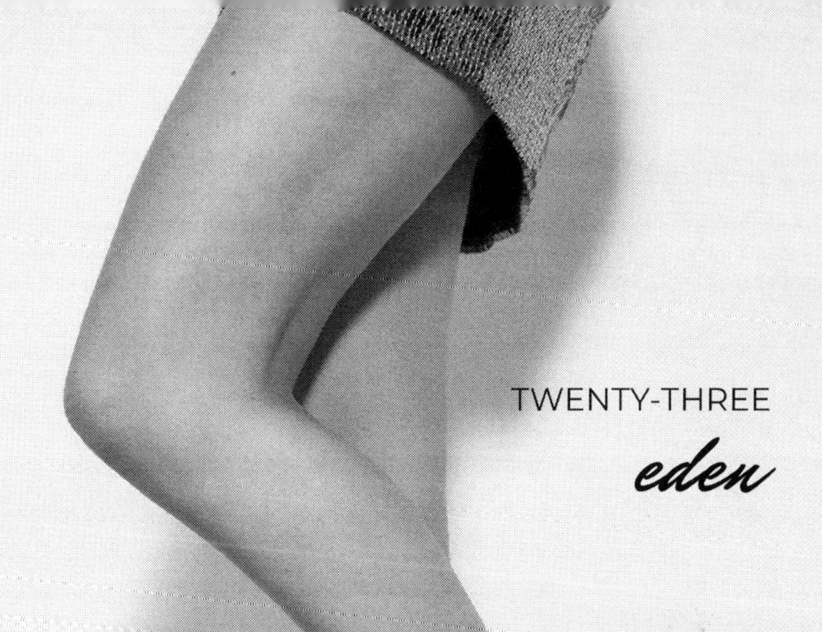

TWENTY-THREE
eden

THE BALLROOM of the hotel resembles an anthill.

People from the catering company, hotel staff, and my company staff move all over the place setting up the last-minute touches.

I wear a headset, listening in on various conversations that are happening between different groups setting up.

Only a few minor blips have occurred so far, but they've been easy to fix. So far, everyone who needs to be here is here or en route.

Except Chase and that has my stomach in knots.

I'm still stunned by the turn of events over the last few days.

Just days after I left Cape Sands, Liz called me to let me know that Chase would be the speaker if I still needed one.

At that point, I'd been desperate, not knowing how I was going to explain to my clients that I still had no keynote speaker.

So, in spite of the fact that I'm still raw emotionally, I agreed to whatever his terms were, which had been surprisingly few.

Eden the professional is doing the happy dance and wishes Chase would hurry up and arrive.

But Eden the woman is riddled with nerves and isn't ready to see him.

I'm not sure I ever will be.

I lay a hand on my stomach, hoping to loosen the knots that are so tight in my gut it's painful.

"DJ is two minutes out," Katie's voice comes through the headset.

"Copy that," I respond.

I blow out a breath and focus back on my job. I haven't come this far to screw it all up now.

With a tablet in hand, I click off a couple of boxes on my checklist and scan the room.

I find one of the waitstaff putting out the wrong silverware and rush to correct it.

I'm walking away to check sound when my cell phone rings and Liz's name pops up.

My gut clenches seeing her name across my screen.

If Chase has changed his mind last minute on being the speaker, I am so screwed.

And so is he because I'll kill him with my bare hands in his fancy-ass house.

Swiping at the screen, I plaster a smile on my face even if she can't see me. "Hey, Liz. How is everything?"

"Hey, Eden. It's fine."

"Good. I haven't seen Chase yet. Is he here?"

"He's on his way, but before he gets here, I need to speak to you in private. Can you meet me in the Presidential suite?"

"Now?"

My incredulous tone must make its way into my voice because she says, "Please. I know you have a million things to do before the start of the event, but I just need a minute of your time."

I rub a hand across my forehead, almost knocking myself out with the tablet.

Maybe that's what I need. To be knocked out. Just wake me up when it's all over.

I sigh and my voice is tight when I speak. "Yes, that's fine. I'll be up in a few minutes."

"Thanks so much. I really appreciate it. I wouldn't ask if it weren't important."

"Right. I'll see you in a few."

I look around and spot Katie coming into the ballroom, waving her down.

"Hey." She blows a piece of hair out of her face before looking me up and down. "I haven't seen you since you changed. You look amazing. That dress is banging."

I roll my eyes and chuckle. "Thanks."

"What's up?"

With a heavy sigh, I pull off my headset and give it and the tablet to her. "Liz called me. I need to go see her for a few minutes upstairs. Can you hang on to that for me, please? I'll be back as soon as I can. Also, can you find someone to check the sound? That needs to be done ASAP."

"I'm on it."

We rush off our separate ways, and I quickly make my way out into the lobby.

Rubbing my temples, I pace the small hallway area outside the elevators, doing my best to tamp down the worry that makes my blood run cold.

I pray that Chase isn't going to screw me over.

We didn't exactly part ways on the best of terms.

That seems like our MO.

This time around though, things had gone so well. We'd opened up to each other. He talked like he'd wanted me, wanted us.

But apparently, I'd lost my ability to read the man.

What am I saying? I've never been able to read Chase Hanover.

It's the whole reason he broke my heart in the first damn place. Not once, but twice.

God, I'm such a fool.

A muted ding signals the elevator, and thankfully the car is empty and no one joins me. I press the button to the top floor where the Presidential suite is located and lean against the wall.

I want to close my eyes, but if I do, I'll probably fall asleep standing. Insomnia has ruled my world since returning to New York.

Instead, I scrutinize my appearance in the mirrored walls of the elevator.

I might be working, but since I'll be presenting the speaker to the crowd, I have to dress the part.

The dress is an oldie but a goodie and makes me feel sexy. The deep emerald-green strapless dress brings out the green in my eyes, stops just above the knee, and the wraparound style of it hugs my curves and creates new ones in all the right places.

I put my hair up on top of my head in an elegantly messy bun to show off the diamond-and-emerald teardrop earrings that were once my mother's.

They're the nicest thing she ever gave me, and she had to die for that to happen.

I'm not blind to the looks I've received from the men in the room. And after the last week or so since I left Cape Sands, I need something to make me feel like a woman again.

Katie's right—my dress is banging.

It's the only thing banging in my world lately.

The red digital numbers on the elevator climb higher while my vision blurs.

I still have no idea how I'm going to face Chase tonight. I haven't spoken to him since the day I left the island.

All of our correspondence in dealing with the speaking engagement has gone through Liz. He's never called or texted me once.

I have to face the fact that the man who owns my heart doesn't want it.

He doesn't want me.

He'd rather hide in his misery and in the past than have a future with me. There's nothing I can say or do to change that.

I just wish my head and my heart could land on the same page.

I finally make it to the top floor, and before the doors open, I dab under my eyes to clear any evidence of tears and not smear the makeup I worked so hard on.

Shoulders back, head up. You can do this, Eden.

At the rate things are going, I won't see Chase until absolutely necessary.

My stride is purposeful and confident as I walk to the double doors at the end of the hallway.

When they both open, my heart meets my heels.

Chase stands on the other side, looking better than any man has a right to in a charcoal-gray suit. The stark white of the button-down shirt and the bright red tie offset his tan skin.

I pray I'm not drooling.

And I don't want to think about what we'd been doing the last time I saw that tie.

His smile turns my insides to liquid. "Eden. Come in."

He stands off to the side, and in a daze, I cross the threshold.

But with each step I take into the suite, my courage strengthens. The doors click shut behind us, and I turn around to face him.

With one hand in his pocket and the other rubbing his chin, he walks toward me, his green eyes shining.

I lift my chin as he gets closer, not wanting him to see how he affects me, even though my heart races, and I can barely catch my breath.

Chase stops in front of me, and his gaze travels from the top of my bun to the tips of my heels.

Heat blooms in my belly, and it's all I can do to keep my knees from buckling when he's so close to me.

I can smell his cologne and the scent that's just...Chase.

How does one explain pheromones?

"Eden, my God. You look..." He blows out a breath. "You take my breath away."

My eyes flick away from his for a moment. "Thank you."

I clear my throat, trying to gain some footing. I don't know what the hell to do with my hands, so I clasp them in front of me. "What are you doing here? I'm supposed to meet Liz."

He looks at me from under his lashes, his thumb rubbing his lower lip. A tiny smile plays on those lips that make me remember too many things I'd rather forget. "Yeah, that was me."

I jerk my head back. "Why would you do that?"

"Because I wasn't sure you'd talk to me after the way I treated you."

I scoff. "Of course I would have talked to you. We have a business arrangement."

"I don't mean professionally. You're the consummate professional. You wouldn't have shut me out there." He pauses, his intense emerald-green gaze on me. "I meant just you and me."

The way he says "you and me" makes a million tiny wildfires ignite in my blood.

But I can't say he's wrong.

If he'd contacted me, I may have told him to fuck off and hung up.

He broke my heart—worse this time because it isn't just young love—and I miss the hell out of him, but I'm not going to let him walk all over me.

"I don't have time for this, Chase." I start toward the door and almost make it, but he's quick.

He steps between me and the door, his back against it. "I'm sorry I brought you up here under false pretenses, but I need to talk to you. And I didn't know any other way." He sighs. "Look, give me five minutes. Just five. After that, you can walk out that door and never give me another thought if that's how you feel. Please?"

There's no playful tone or dancing eyes to his plea, as if he's saying it just to get to me.

No, the only thing I see in his eyes is hope.

Damn it, it'd be easier to tell him to shove it if he were joking around. But that hopeful look tugs at my delicate heartstrings.

Not to mention, he's just too damn close to me.

I step back. "Fine. Five minutes. Say what you need to say."

"I love you."

My eyes narrow. "Oh, really? But love isn't enough. Isn't that what you told me?"

"Yeah, but I was wrong."

I blink. "Come again?"

"I said I was wrong." He closes his eyes and thumps his head back on the door. "Blurting out 'I love you' isn't the first thing I wanted to say, but as usual I can't seem to think straight when you're so close to me."

Join the club, buddy.

He opens his eyes and looks down at me. "The first thing I wanted to say was I'm sorry. I acted like a total asshole the day you left. And while it doesn't excuse my behavior, I need you to know why I acted that way."

I cross my arms over my chest and lift a brow. "Go on."

His gaze wanders down my body, all the way to my toes, before snapping back to my stare. "God, you're just so...stunning. I can't think."

He runs a hand through his hair, and I have to steel myself against any more compliments until he says his piece.

"I was scared. Plain and simple. Relationships with people I love have never gone well. And whenever I fall for someone, or even get the notion that I'm falling for someone, I hear my father's voice in my head telling me I'm going to hurt them just like I did my mother. It's why I didn't fight for you, for us, all those years ago. I thought that since I'd eventually hurt you somehow anyway, I was going to let you go before that happened."

He blows out a breath and looks out over my head. "And with everything that happened with Heather...it just reinforced what I'd been told since I was fourteen years old." His gaze comes back to me. "That I was a selfish bastard that didn't deserve to be loved."

My heart breaks for the young boy who not only lost his mother he'd adored, but then was blamed for her death by his father.

The one person left that should have protected him.

I want to reach out and hug him and the man he's become. The good man he can't see he is.

My fingers tighten around my biceps to keep from

throwing myself at him. Because I need more. But I also want to offer some comfort.

"Chase, you didn't kill your mother. Or Heather."

He nods and looks down. "I know. But I've lived with his voice in my head for so long, it's almost comforting in a weird-ass way."

His head lifts and he looks me in the eye. "But then you came to the island, and you knocked me to my knees. You were in that red skirt and heels, and I wanted you so badly, but at the same time, you reminded me of New York and all the reasons I'd left the city behind."

I tilt my head, and my brow furrows. "And yet, here you are. Why? What changed with the whole media thing?"

"I'm here for you. Because of you, Eden. I'm fighting for you this time. I'm fighting for us. I don't want the media to run my life anymore when they don't give a shit about me anyway. I don't want to live in that house all by myself anymore. And I don't want to go another day without waking up with you next to me."

My heart thunders in my chest. After being with Chase again, this time around isn't so easy to get over him.

For him to be here, saying these things...it's really all I've ever wanted when it comes to love.

He moves closer, and for the life of me, I can't move. I'm mesmerized by that deep baritone of his voice.

"I love you, Eden. I'm willing to do whatever I need to do to show you that. In fact,"—his lips curve in a smile—"I started going to therapy."

My eyes widen. "You did?"

"And I got a cat. Well, a kitten really."

"You have a cat?"

He nods once. "I do. And her name is Freyja."

"Why Freyja?"

He grins. "I wanted something strong and all I could think about was you. But I didn't want to name her Eden. Then I got to thinking about when we met in literature class and we were learning mythology. And when we learned about Freyja, all I could think about is you."

My heart skips a beat. "You never told me that."

"She was the Norse goddess of love, sex, beauty, fertility, magic. All the things you are, Eden."

Holy shit. I'm so stunned, I can't even speak.

He takes advantage of my speechlessness and continues. "Listen, I'm not fixed or totally healed. But I'm working on it. Because I don't want to be alone anymore. I want to be with you. You make me want to be a better man, Eden. The kind of man you deserve, though I'm not sure any man is good enough to deserve you. But I'll spend the rest of my life trying to be. If you'll let me."

Tears blur my vision, and I focus on the red tie. I run a hand down it, the warmth of his skin radiating through it, his heart beating fast underneath it.

"I'm scared too, Chase. I can't be hurt by you again. I won't survive it." I look up at him and find his stare full of love and hope. "How do I know you won't hurt me again?"

He lowers his forehead to mine and lifts his hands to my hips. "Love is full of ups and downs, hurt and happiness. I can't guarantee that I'll never do anything that will hurt you. But I can guarantee that I will love you for the rest of my life, and if I do hurt you, I'll do whatever I have to do to make it right. We'll work it out. There's no more running, no more pushing each other away."

I bite my lip to keep from bursting into tears. "That's all I've ever wanted from you, Chase. To have the chance to love each other through the good and the bad. Because I love you too."

He brings his hands up to cup my face. "Eden, it's always been you. I've been lost for the last decade without you. I don't want to be apart from you again."

"Then don't."

I yank on his tie, bringing his mouth to mine.

He spins me around, and my back hits the wall as his kiss turns those tiny wildfires into a blazing inferno. My hands roam over the fabric of his suit, searching for purchase.

He presses his hard body into mine, and I want him to take me right there up against the door.

As I start to unbutton his suit jacket to push it off his shoulders, his phone pings from his pocket.

We break apart, our chests heaving. "That's our cue," he says.

My head is foggy, and I just want more of him. "What?" My head clears and my eyes widen. "Oh my God, I don't have my phone. What time is it?"

He chuckles. "I told Katie to text me when it was time for us to head down."

"Katie knew you were here?"

He nods with a grin. "Yep. By the way,"—he points at my hair—"you need to check your hair before we head down. You look like a woman who was almost fucked against the door."

A hand flies to my hair and my eyes widen. I rush to the bathroom and survey the damage. "Damn it. I can't look like we just had sex!"

He leans against the doorjamb, looking none the worse for wear. "Well, we didn't."

I redo the bobby pins in my hair, smoothing out the flyaways. "How is it you look normal?"

"Oh sweetheart, I have the jacket to help me. Just don't laugh if I'm hobbling down the hall."

We laugh, and our eyes meet in the mirror. I turn to him and he pulls me close. "I love you, Eden. Heart and soul."

"I love you too, Chase. Heart and soul."

Our kiss is sweet and tender but starts to edge toward hot. We pull away before we really do miss the event.

"Ready for this?" I ask.

His hand slides into mine, and he kisses the back of it. "I'm ready for anything with you next to me."

epilogue

EDEN

Six Months Later

I PULL my car through the gates of what is now not just Chase's house, but our home.

It's early—just barely past sunrise—and I smile as I look out over the purple skies and the dark blue water.

I'd changed my flight time on the charter jet Chase arranged for me so I could surprise him. Exhaustion is heavy in my bones, but it's counteracted by the exhilaration of seeing my man.

The night of the charity ball had been an unforgettable night in so many ways. Not only had Chase's speech been a huge hit, but the event raised well beyond the goal the guys were looking to hit.

In fact, Hudson, Graham, and Carter want me to host the event annually for them.

I agreed.

The money my company made off the event not only put us back in the black but allowed me to pay off some of the outstanding business loans.

Chase and I did our best to make up for lost time by holing up in the Presidential suite for three days.

But then it was time to get back to reality, and Chase headed back to Cape Sands, but we'd made plans for me to fly down the following weekend.

I flew down and never went back.

Well, that's not true.

I did go back to pack my apartment up and turn my keys in.

My job is one that can be done anywhere, so I gave my employees the option to work from home or in the office. We all meet at the office once a month to review upcoming events.

The fact I have a team I trust to be my eyes and ears in New York made the move to Florida easy.

In fact, I promoted Katie to vice president and she runs the New York office. The team loves her, and she's dedicated to the business.

With Charley's help and connections in Cape Sands, I now have a Florida office as well, offering event services in Cape Sands.

I already have a couple of weddings scheduled for spring of next year.

I leave my suitcase in the car and creep inside quietly.

Freyja wraps her little but growing body around my legs.

"Hey, sweet girl. I missed you."

I snuggle with her for a moment before setting her on the floor and tiptoeing into the bedroom.

God, I missed him. I was gone a bit longer than normal this time—ten days—and while we'd had phone sex every night, it just wasn't the same.

When I walk into the room, I stop and just stare at him.

I can't believe that sexy man is mine.

He lies face up in the center of the bed, one arm over his head, the other resting on his chest. The sheet is pulled up to his waist, leaving his chest bare but covering one of my favorite body parts.

The white of the sheet is stark against his tanned skin, and a five o'clock shadow darkens his strong jaw.

I bite my lip in anticipation of feeling that beard burn against the inside of my thighs.

Toeing off my shoes in the shadows, I grin as I quickly shed down to nothing and slide under the covers with him.

His skin warm under my touch, I brush a hand over his chest.

I lift the sheet and peek under it, my small grin turning into a full-blown one, heat rushing between my legs.

He isn't at full staff yet, but he's getting there, and my thighs clench at the sight of his piercing that makes me wild.

I drop soft kisses on his neck and shoulder, causing him to moan and shift slightly, but he doesn't wake up.

Pursing my lips, I eye his profile, wondering why he hasn't moved yet.

The kisses I drop this time aren't as soft, and I nip at his ear, my gaze on the area under the sheet that begins to tent.

But still he doesn't move.

When I bring my gaze back to look at him, those beautiful green eyes are on me.

Lust, love, and a dash of humor dance in his eyes.

Before I can take my next breath, Chase flips me on my back and stretches out over me. My wrists are in one of his hands and pulled above my head.

I'm completely bare to his gaze, and everywhere he looks makes me feel like he's branding me.

His lips curve into a smile. "Well, well. Isn't this a pleasant way to wake up in the morning?" He slants his mouth over mine and kisses me with such intensity, my toes tingle.

"Surprise," I murmur against his mouth.

Chase

Surprise indeed.

The last ten days have been hell on earth without Eden with me.

The only thing that got me through and kept me from being a total grumpy bastard—besides the nightly phone sex —is knowing that when she came back, she was staying.

There's nothing stopping us from being together.

I buck my hips, rubbing my hard length against her, her moans and mewls burning me from the inside out.

She arches against me, pleading for me to fuck her.

Who am I to turn that down?

When I slide into her wet pussy, we groan at finally being able to come together after the torturous foreplay over the last ten days.

I drive into her, and she wraps her legs around my waist, meeting my thrusts.

The way we move together always makes me push harder, the feeling of love so big in my chest, I think it might burst.

Her core muscles clench around me, and she tightens her thighs around my waist, putting me in that vise grip I love.

We come at the same time with such intensity, I swear the top of my head blows off.

And it's like that every time.

I'm a lucky, lucky man.

I shift off her and gather her against me.

She snuggles into my side, and there's no place I'd rather be than right here with her for the rest of my days.

But there's something I need to do, and I can't think of a better time.

"I have something to tell you."

"Okay, tell me."

"Well, first you need to sit up and close your eyes."

"Ooooh...I'm intrigued."

She sits up, eyes closed, a beautiful smile on her face.

From my nightstand drawer, I pull out the black velvet box that I've been waiting to give her for the last week.

I pop it open and say, "Okay, open your eyes."

Her eyes open and she looks down at the ring I hold up. Immediately, tears fill her eyes. "Oh, Chase..."

I'll remember how she looks at this moment—turquoise eyes wide and shining, that beautiful pink flush to her skin from our recent bout of sex, her blonde hair a sexy mess—for the rest of my life.

"Eden Mitchell, you are the best thing in my life. I want to kiss you awake, and be the last person you talk to before you go to sleep. I want to watch you nurse our children, knowing that you and I created a life together in all the ways that matter most. I want to love you until my days on this earth are done. Will you do me the honor of becoming my wife?"

The ring glints in the early morning sun, but it has nothing on the light in Eden's blue-green eyes.

She nods and covers her mouth. "Yes, yes, I'll marry you, Chase."

I slide the large solitaire on her finger and cup her face in my hands. "I love you, Eden. Thank you for bringing me back to life."

Her smile is shaky, and tears run down her cheeks. "I love you, Chase. Thank you for loving me."

My lips meet hers, sealing the deal and making her mine forever.

Want to see Chase and Eden in the future? Check out the bonus chapter here or scan the code below.

. . .

epilogue 2

LUCAS

"WHEN WILL Lucas Raines return to baseball? The thirty-nine-year-old veteran pitcher is on the injured list—"

Click.

"Raines was put on the injured list in late April after he left the game in the seventh inning against the Mets, after experiencing tightness in his forearm and was unable to throw. He—"

Click.

"Larry, do you think Raines will be able to return to baseball after having Tommy John surgery?"

The pretty blonde newscaster turns to her balding, overweight, co-host Larry Gordon, who isn't a fan of mine.

A little smirk plays across his lips before he speaks, making my blood boil.

Asshole.

"It's hard to say. I think he's been putting it off for years, and it finally came back to bite him."

"Fuck you, Larry," I mutter under my breath, but dread curls in my gut.

"And even if he comes back, it's doubtful he'll ever have that perfect game he's chasing."

It's a well-aimed shot below the belt, and he knows it.

Being the mature adult I am, I give the oversized TV screen the finger.

My legs bounce, nerves and anxiety making my insides quiver. They're two concepts foreign to me until now, and I have no idea how to handle it.

Unable to sit any longer, I stand and begin to pace the small, plush waiting area of the Bull Sharks training facility.

"You're going to wear a hole in the carpet."

I turn to see Nate come up behind me, a smile on his face. I run my good hand through my hair and blow out a breath. I'm glad to see he's alone.

I didn't need "losing my fucking mind" added to the list of my defects right now.

A dead arm is more than enough.

I come to a stop in front of him. "Sorry."

"I'm just giving you shit." He glances at the screen. "Ah, Larry Gordon. Still pissed at you for that time he said you purposely hit him with a pitch and the ump didn't agree?"

I rub the back of my neck, where it seems the tension has decided to permanently reside. "Seems so."

Nate crosses his arms over his chest, his gaze on the TV. "He went on to strike out and, in the next inning, collided with the wall and broke his leg, ending his career."

"He holds a grudge, apparently." I sigh before turning to him. "What are you doing here? I thought you'd be down at the stadium by now."

"I heard you're starting PT today, so I thought I'd come and check on you before you started."

Before Nate retired and then came back to work in the club's front office, we'd started as a battery 310 times, one of the longest runs as a pitcher and catcher combo in league history.

Besides my buddy Theo, Nate is the closest thing I have to a brother.

"Thanks, man. But I'm fine."

He raises a brow. "You sure?"

I know what he's asking without asking.

How's your mental game?

My gut churns at the insinuation. Baseball is a mentally challenging sport, and my head needs to be as right as my arm.

Clearing my throat, I look back to the TV, where a commercial for a high-end whiskey has replaced Larry the asshole.

Rolling my lips inward, I nod. "Yeah, I'm good." I feel the weight of his stare on me. "Okay, I'm working on it."

My phone pings, and I bite back a sigh of relief.

Relief that's short-lived when I read the text on the screen.

THEO: Hey man. I need to talk to you. Text me when you get a chance today.

My stomach drops at the urgent tone of his text. It's not normal for Theo. But I don't have time to do more than fire back a quick response.

ME: Headed into PT. Text back after.

A thumbs-up emoji pops up, and I slide my phone back into my pocket.

Before I can reassure Nate that I'm indeed just fine, a door opens behind me. Nate grins, dropping his voice to where only I can hear him. "It appears you've got the new PT on staff for your rehab."

When I turn to face the therapist who's going to be my best

friend and worst enemy for the next several weeks, my ears begin to ring.

My brain quits working and I'm rendered speechless.

It's the same fucking reaction every time I see her.

The woman I spent a weekend with that still plays rent free in my head.

The woman who has owned my heart for a decade.

The woman who ruined me.

The only one in the world off-limits to me. Not because she works for the Bull Sharks but because she's Evelyn Taylor.

My best friend Theo's sister.

The sister I swore whose heart I'd never break.

And then I did.

What can you expect from Forbidden Forever?

- Second chance
- Age gap
- Brother's best friend
- Forbidden workplace trysts
- It's always been you
- Small town sports
- He fell first
- Hate to want you
- That "fuck it" moment
- Mementos from the past

Pre-order here or scan the QR code below!

get a sneak peake of all things eliza!

If you'd like exclusive content, first look at cover reveals, bonus material and other announcements first, join my newsletter, The Sneak Peake!

Want all the book fun in a drama free zone? Join my reader group, Eliza's Sassy Belles. We have a fun group going and growing all the time!

also by eliza peake

The Cape Sands Series

(Standalone Spicy, Small Town Sports Romances)

Unexpected Forever

Mine Forever

Forbidden Forever - Coming Spring 2025

* * *

The Madison Ridge Series: Homecoming

(Standalone Steamy, Small Town Romances)

Trouble Me

Remind Me

Wreck Me

Unexpected Christmas

* * *

Love's Kaleidoscope

A unique collection of love themed short stories.

* * *

NONFICTION

30 Days Until "The End": An Inspirational Guide to Finishing Your Novel in 30 Days

If you're looking for humor, positivity, and a swift kick to your flagging motivation, Eliza Peake's inspirational guide to completing a draft in thirty days is a must have.

acknowledgments

Some of you may have read this book when it was Tormented Bastard as part of the Cocky Hero World.

It didn't get much visibility, but then in May 2024, I got the rights back to it and I was so happy about it. Per my contract with CHW, I had to make some changes anyway, so I thought, Chase would fit in nicely with my other baseball guys.

I've always loved Chase. He was just so broken and I wanted to just hug him in spite of his prickly exterior. And I wanted so badly to get their story out into the world and Mine Forever was born.

The core of the story is the same, but the changes I've made just enhanced what the story was before and it's better than ever now.

With all the changes I made, I'm giving my editors Ann Riza and Ann Suhs at Happily Editing Ann's a special shout out. They were so patient with me when I sent this to them and then still made more changes. A huge thank you for catching all those things I didn't and making sure everything made sense! Y'all really are the best in the business and I love you.

Thank you to Julianne Fangmann at Heart to Cover for the title and cover formatting and Christiana Theocleous at Concepts by Canea for knowing exactly what I wanted with the illustrated cover. You two are my cover masters!

Also, Christiana, thank you for being such an amazing beta reader that's honest and making me a better writer.

I'd be remiss if I didn't thank Tiffany Hernandez, Richelle Emory, Jackie Walker, Melissa Ivers, Lilian Harris, the Sassy Belles, my ARC team, bookstagrammers and bloggers who all took a chance on me at some point.

To Mr. P and Nat for always supporting me, promoting me, and cheering me on when I'm feeling doubtful. I love y'all so much!

TO THE READERS!!! I can't thank y'all enough!! This dream I have of telling stories and sharing them with the world is nothing without you guys.

And to God, for blessing me with all I have.

XOXO

Eliza

about the author

Eliza Peake is an international bestselling author of sexy, small town contemporary romance. She writes stories with smart, saucy heroines, charming, swoonworthy heroes who love their women in all the right ways, and happily ever afters with all the feels.

In her downtime, she reads all the panty-melting romances she can get her hands on, drinks gallons of coffee, and tries to wrangle her addiction to Mexican food.

She currently resides in North Georgia with her family and dreams of retiring to the beach someday where she will continue writing steamy romance stories to her heart's content.

www.elizapeake.com

Made in the USA
Columbia, SC
11 March 2025

71273ae8-505f-4d80-99d2-c18955291860R01